Heart & Home

Book One : Langdon Trilogy

By

Susan Elle

For

Ursula Publishing UK

Heart & Home

Book One : Langdon Trilogy

Text Copyright © 2014

By Susan Elle

Ursula Publishing UK

All Rights Reserved.

Cover Photograph

Kevin Eaves © /Dreamstime.com

ISBN 978-1-910753-21-7

<u>Other Books by Susan Elle</u>

The Sara Colson Trilogy includes
Sara's Child
Sara's Loss
Sara's Shame
All the above also available as audio books.

Catherine Colson-Sayers Investigations
CCS Investigations : Bk 1 : Missing
CCS Investigations : Bk 2 : The Chosen
CCS Investigations : Bk 3 : Travis
CCS Investigations : Bk 4 : Deleted
CCS Investigations : Bk 5 : Mind Games, due out end
Aug 2015, twice the length of previous books.

Tempest
Broken

Love, Lies & Consequences Trilogy
Love : Bk1
Lies : Bk2
Consequences : Bk3

Langdon Trilogy
Heart & Home : Bk1
Heart of a Lion : Bk2
Heart of Stone : Bk3

www.susan-elle.com

TABLE OF CONTENTS

<u>PROLOGUE</u>

I don't know who it was that said 'be careful what you wish for' but I now understand the meaning behind those frivolous words.

My name is Matt Langdon, short for Matthias and I'm the second of three children born to Avis and Charles Langdon. My elder brother, Chadwick — and if anyone dares to call him that he'll flatten them or glare so damned hard he'll fry their insides — has gone missing in action. At least, that's how I think of him. And then there's Ashton, my little sister — she's the most stubborn individual I have ever known. At 16 she's starting to get some unwelcome attention — unwelcome from my point of view, that is.

My parents are retired and Chad and I were running the farm and minding our little sister, until Chad disappeared recently after getting his heart broken – not that he'd admit that in a million years. But now it seems I've got what I always wished for – the farm is mine to do with what I think is right and I don't have to run everything by Chad all the damn time.

Trouble is, there's so much to do and Ashton is becoming a real handful. She's just finished school and when her exam results come out they're expected to be aces. She has a good brain, but Ashton has decided that the farm is going to be her career and she doesn't need fancy A-levels or a degree to do what she's been doing all her life.

If Chad were here he'd be on her case and Ashton wouldn't dare go against him. Well...she would, but it wouldn't get her anywhere. Once Chad has his mind made up about something you're better off skipping the protests, the wasted arguments, and get on with doing what 'he' wants.

It seems like Chad has always ruled Langdon farm – even when we were growing up, dad seemed to defer to his ideas. Just little things, at first – like when he decided that I was old enough, at ten, to be mucking out the stables with a little supervision from Mac, a long time trusted farm hand; and Ashton, at 6, ought to be learning how to sweep the stable yard and do general tidying up.

There's four years between each one of us, and Chad had only been fourteen when he advised our dad that bringing in a certain kind of new technology for milking the cows would quickly pay for itself with a greater yield – and I have to admit, the old system was slow and no doubt didn't do as good a job...but I've never admitted as much to Chad, he's got a big enough head as it is!

And I suppose he did a good enough job of sourcing a better feed price a few years ago – now I'm running the show I get to see the books and study them, he saved us a pretty penny back then.

Now all I have to do is live up to 'the big man's' previous good record and not let the farm go to rack and ruin – not such an easy task in these testing economic times.

CHAPTER ONE

As I walked across to the stable yard I heard Chad's horse protesting loudly, no doubt unhappy at not being ridden in a while.

"What the hell are you doing?!" I demanded, watching pale faced as Ashton swung herself up into the saddle of Chad's horse. "Ronan is far too strong headed for you to ride – Chad told you never to go near him, let alone try to ride him – now get the hell down and I'll get Mac to help you get him back inside!"

But as I strode away to the tack-room on my right, Ashton clicked her tongue, urging Ronan out of the stable yard. Swinging back around, I shouted after her, "Ashton, damn it – get back here!"

But Ashton disappeared and the moment Ronan felt his hooves planted on the grassy field next to the stables he took off like a greyhound let out of a trap.

Not the least bit afraid, Ashton gave the Arab stallion his head and charged through a chill wind that met them head on. But she was too excited to feel its bite and the stallion flexed his muscles after being cooped up in his stable for the last couple of days.

"Steady, Ronan...," Aston shouted to be heard above the wind, "...steady boy!"

But Ronan didn't pay her any heed, not when she tried to calm him with her voice or when she tried to turn him and head back towards the stables.

They crossed a lot of land and a fence bordering the neighbouring farm was looming large on their horizon.

"Ronan, stop, damn it!" But no matter what she did Ronan kept going and Ashton had to accept that they were going to jump the fence.

With his nostrils flaring and his blond mane whipping back in the wind, Ronan didn't hesitate, but took the fence like he was jumping barrels in the training ring, and still he didn't stop.

From the corner of her green eyes, Ashton could see movement that appeared to be getting nearer, but she didn't dare loose her concentration, even for a moment, to look at what it might be.

A large black horse was gaining ground on them, but

only after Ronan and Ashton had taken another fence in their stride and the stallion began to tire.

Wesley Craemer brought his horse alongside Ashton, shouting across to make sure that she was alright.

"I'm fine..." she protested stubbornly, "...go away!"

But her arms were tiring and her legs were really feeling the strain of keeping her seated on the runaway stallion's back.

"I'm going to get a little ahead of you then gently turn to the left and hopefully bring Ronan to a stop, or at least slow him down," Wesley told her, ignoring her scathing glare. "Get ready," he warned, then manoeuvred to carry out his plan.

"Come on, Titan, let's show him we're here," he shouted to his horse, and urged him forward and nearer to Ronan's head.

Giving Ronan time to take in the fact that he now had company, Wesley eventually began to steer Titan over to the left, cutting off Ronan's headlong galloping stride and steering him towards the river that ran through his father's land.

But Ronan still had some excess energy to burn off and, although his stride was hampered and his progress slowed, the Arab stallion seemed determined not to stop for anyone or anything.

Still riding at his head, Wesley continued to steer Titan in a gradual left turn and his horse seemed to understand what was going on and cooperated fully. When Ronan tried to nudge his way past him, Titan stretched his neck out and butted his head against the wayward stallion's nose not allowing him to gain any ground.

"Good boy," Wesley encouraged, his head bent low over Titan's long black mane. And then the river loomed in the near distance and Wesley looked across at Ashton and realised that she was tiring badly. "Come on, Titan, give it all you've got!"

Forcing his horse harder into Ronan's path, the rebellious stallion had no option but to turn more abruptly to its left and the river was now straight ahead.

"Wesley!" Ashton screamed when she realised his plan. "You maniac!"

The river had risen due to recent heavy rainfalls and when Ronan plunged into it Ashton tried hard to hang on to his reins but quickly found herself flailing around in the river and then being hauled ungraciously to her feet.

Watching her cough and splutter, Wesley asked if she was ok, then took a step back when her green eyes turned on him, full of humiliation and anger.

"Of course I'm not alright," Ashton screamed at him. "You could have drowned me, you moron!"

Standing waist deep in cold water, the thin yellow t-shirt she had thought very fashionable that morning was now virtually transparent and doing nothing to hide her heaving breasts from Wesley's admiring gaze.

"Stop throwing a fit," he told her with an indulgent grin. Wesley Craemer had been a friend to Ashton's brothers for as long as he could remember. They used to hang around together as boys and, until recently, the three men would go for drinks in the nearby village together.

But that was before Chad had split up with Wesley's sister, Fallon. He'd asked Chad what the hell did he see in her – ok she's pretty enough, Wesley had conceded, but she's contrary and as high spirited as the horses she rides.

Now Chad was gone and Fallon had been in a foul mood since the day he took off – just like Chad's sister was right now, in fact.

"Here..." Wesley held out a hand to Ashton, "...let me help you."

But Ashton angrily batted it aside, raising a haughty chin in the air to brush past him. And she almost made it, but her foot slid on a rock and she toppled sideways, arms shooting out to grab onto anything that would halt her progress back into the water that was already up to her waist.

"Shit!" Ashton gasped, then found herself hauled against Wesley, his hard muscled arms circling her like unyielding iron restraints.

"Will you stop being so damned stubborn," he chided none too gently, working hard to stop her from squirming free of him and drowning herself, and him, in the river. "Damn it, Ashton, stay still!"

Then suddenly she did, her breath coming in gasps and her green eyes gazing up at him warily.

His eyes held Ashton's, his breathing as uneven as hers but for a very different reason. All her squirming against him had given Wesley a hard on that he could do little to hide – and Ashton was looking up at him in dazed anticipation.

"God damn it, Ashton, don't look at me like that," he warned, trying to put her from him.

But for some reason that Ashton didn't understand, she didn't want him to let her go and moved back into his arms, her lips parted...wanting...waiting...and then her tongue flicked over them in an innocent movement that drove Wesley over the edge of reason.

Grabbing a handful of long red hair, Wesley tugged her head back and crushed Ashton's tender, inexperienced lips in a kiss that rocked them both.

For Ashton it was shocking, the assault on her young

body so profound that it frightened her...then roused her enough to begin returning the kiss, her hand reaching up to cup the back of Wesley's head pulling him down harder.

When his hand moved roughly over her breast, Ashton didn't pull away but arched her back in an effort to give him more, only aware that she needed Wesley in ways that were making her ache in places she'd never ached in before.

And then he was gone – plunging head first into the cold river Wes stayed under for the longest time.

Scanning the water, desperate for any sign of him, Ashton called out his name, fear in her voice when Wesley didn't immediately resurface.

When she felt her elbow taken in a firm grip, Ashton tried to wheel round to see the man who was now steering her roughly towards the river bank.

"What the hell...?"

"Shut up, Ashton!" Wesley was furious, with her and most assuredly with himself. What the hell was he thinking – Ashton was like a little sister to him, the nuisance child always trying to tag along when he and her brothers had tried ditching her to get into some mischief or other.

For christ's sake, she's 16 and I'm 22 – enough said!

The two large horses were companionably standing together munching on grass, no hint of the recent drama in their outwardly peaceful demeanour.

"What's wrong?" Ashton tried to look up at Wesley, uncertain and, for some reason, afraid.

But he didn't answer or look at Ashton, continuing to virtually drag her towards the horses that had raised their heads in mild interest at their approach.

"I'll help you up onto Titan – he's got more sense than Ronan so you'll be safe enough," Wesley stated abruptly.

But Ashton was recovering herself, feeling foolish and rejected by Wesley treating her like a child.

"I can take Ronan back," she stated mutinously, and shrugged her elbow out of Wesley's grasp then made to step around him.

"Haven't you learned anything today?!" Wesley ground out between gritted teeth, his fury barely hidden as he halted her progress by grasping her arm.

Suddenly Ashton's flare of temper evaporated and there were tears in her eyes when she looked up at Wesley.

"You're hurting me," she told him, not sure if she was talking about her arm or her heart, and for a long moment Wesley just stared down at her.

"I could hurt you, Ashton. I could so very easily hurt

you and you wouldn't have the sense to stop me," he told her more gently, taking his hand from her arm and stroking his knuckles down her wet cheek. "Now be a good girl and let me help you up on Titan – we need to get you home."

CHAPTER TWO

One year later.

Horseboxes were grouped together at the rear of the arena – owners and riders talking about the course their horse was about to tackle and the tactics for achieving the fastest clear round.

"Don't try cutting the corner to the triple too sharply – you may shave a fraction of a second off the time but you'll take that first fence down for sure," one of the owners was telling his horse's rider.

"That's good advice," I told Ashton as we walked Fonteyn, a 16 hand piebald mare, towards the competition ring.

Adjusting her riding hat and straightening her navy jacket over pale beige jodhpurs, Ashton gave me a wry sideways look that told me she knew exactly what she was doing.

Cupping my hands together to give her a boost up into the saddle, I grinded. "So, I'm only good for stepping on," I chided her playfully.

"Of course," Ashton agreed returning my grin. "Now make sure you do your job and watch my round carefully. When I get through to the next round I'll need all your tips and tricks to win the ride-off!"

I knew my job and, when her name was called and Ashton entered the ring, I moved to a good vantage point to make notes for improving her next round, as sure as my sister that she would get through this one.

Yes, no, no, take your time, take your time – ok, ok, that's a girl, now let her go... Oh Christ!

"You look like you're about to have a heart attack," Fenella Swain sidled up to my side, her haughty voice distracting me from my task. "Stop acting like a mother hen – Ashton's a big girl, for heaven's sake!" she added when I didn't give her my full attention.

"Just give me a minute..." I told her, still watching Ashton's every move, "...she's only got the triple to go." Then I punched the air as Ashton and Fonteyn flew over the last fence for a clear round and turned to Fenella, taking her in my arms and planting a firm kiss on her astonished pouting lips.

"Aren't they a brilliant team?!" I stated rather than

asked as I put Fenella away from me and watched the duo come into view.

Looking pleased and excited, Ashton guided Fonteyn round the side of our horsebox and dismounted.

"So, what did you think – wasn't she wonderful?" Ashton asked giving her proud mare an appreciative pat on the neck and scratching under her forelock just where she knew Fonteyn liked it.

But before I could congratulate her, Ashton caught sight of Fenella and her smile disappeared.

"She's not a bad jumper – her timing wasn't quite right going into the treble, but that's more to do with the rider's inexperience," Fenella stated before turning on her heels and stalking off.

"Why was *she* here?" Ashton demanded, watching the older woman's receding form and feeling resentful of her gorgeous figure.

"It's just Fenella," I dismissed easily, giving Ashton a 'what's-the-big-deal' shrug. "Let's just go through these notes and concentrate on the next round."

Passing Fonteyn's reins over to Pam, our stable manager, Ashton followed after me.

"I've told you before, she's after you," Ashton frowned after the woman who was no longer visible in the crowd.

Shaking my head at her fancifulness, I chuckled softly as I lead her to the fence. "On the whole you did ok — there were a few turns that you took a bit too tight and you're going to have to watch yourself in the next round — those same fences will be even higher the next time you jump them," I reminded her, pointing to the three fences I was talking about. "You rocked that third one and were lucky it didn't fall — the rest you cleared cleanly."

"If you don't take a few chances you don't win," Ashton pointed out with a lifted brow. "Just look at Erica..." and she wafted a hand at the horse and rider we were currently watching in the ring, "... she'll get through because she rides so carefully but she won't win the competition because she doesn't know how to take a risk."

"Unlike you, hey champ," a familiar voice taunted her from behind them.

Turning, Ashton looked daggers at Wesley Craemer and his latest bit of fluff hanging on his arm. "At least I'm not too scared to compete," she told him somewhat snidely.

"You used to do this?" the dumb blonde on his arm looked up at Wesley as if he was her hero and talked like she was six years old. "But I would love to see my man on top of one of those fine horses — you would look so sexy," she told him, a manicured hand rubbing over his chest.

Giving a firm shake of his head, Wesley smiled down at the woman at his side and wasn't even sure if he remembered her name. "I don't have the time – I like doing lots of other things," he crooned seductively and bent his head to kiss her scarlet painted lips.

"Jesus, get a room!" And after giving Wesley a scathing glare, Ashton marched over to Fonteyn, and Pam who was looking after her.

"You two used to get along," I observed, watching my sister's ram-rod straight spine as she stalked away. "Couldn't you at least try to play nice?"

"Nah, it's more fun this way. And besides, she's the one who takes umbrage every time we meet," Wesley pointed out, but knew that wasn't entirely true.

Ever since he had saved her from Ronan, a headstrong stallion that had bolted with Ashton barely managing to stay seated on his back, the two had been at logger-heads.

Things had suddenly become sexually charged and he had so very nearly lost himself in her. But Ashton had only been 16 and had probably never even been kissed.

But she had returned his kiss with gusto once she had gotten over the shock of him taking her in his arms and kissing her near to senseless. And then things had heated up fast and his hands just couldn't get enough of her, he remembered.

If Matthias had even the slightest idea of what had happened between them, Wesley was sure that he wouldn't be standing here now.

"You're probably right..." I conceded, "...it's probably got something to do with her hormones. She's getting to be a real handful..." I continued, frowning towards my sister's back, "...I wish to God Chad would come home, he'd soon set her straight!"

"Things can't be that bad, surely?" Wesley grinned, but he too looked over at Ashton with some concern.

"Oh can't it," I huffed loudly. "She's always on the phone to some boy or other and she stays out till midnight when she hasn't got a competition she's training for." Shaking my head ruefully, I once again voiced my deepest wish. "Come back Chad, all is forgiven – please!"

The names of those riders through to the final round were announced over the tannoy and I noted that my sister would be third up.

Walking over to where Ashton was still talking to Pam, I made sure that she was aware of the riding order. "You're up third," I stated, making sure that I got my sister's full attention. "Don Craig and Samantha Weston are 1st and 2nd to ride, then you," I reiterated. "Don is just going into the ring so let's go and watch how he does."

Making our way over to the rails, Ashton and I moved to the front and Wesley and the no-name bit of fluff on his arm stood to the back of us.

Feeling tense with Wesley stood right behind her, Ashton found it difficult to concentrate – but then the hooter sounded and the first horse and rider got underway against the clock.

Don cleared the first three fences easily then reined his horse in to prepare for the higher wall. Clipping the top brick with his horse's rear hooves, Don did a swift look back to see if it had fallen, but it was still balancing on the edge. Then he had a sharp turn to negotiate for the water jump and then round to a double and another quick turn for the final triple. And then another hooter sounded to mark the end of a good clear round.

"Don Craig, riding Mr Mercer, has achieved a clear round in 48 seconds – now let's give a warm welcome to Samantha Weston, riding Lord Brown," a disembodied voice announced over the tannoy.

Turning from the fence, Ashton found herself walking into Wesley, he was standing that close. "Sorry," she blushed and tried to push past him, but not before her heart gave a leap and her pulse rate spiked alarmingly.

No matter how much she tried to tell herself that she

didn't even like Wesley Craemer, Ashton couldn't help the effect he always seemed to have on her.

"Not a problem," Wesley assured her, his hands on her arms to steady her. "Just be careful out there..." and he lifted his chin to indicate the ring, "...don't take any stupid risks."

Her green eyes looked questioningly up at him as Ashton tried to work out whether or not he really cared – then she gave a shrug when the bit of fluff moved in to cling more tightly to Wesley's arm.

With her long red hair trailing down her back in a neat braid, Ashton let Matt give her a boost up into the saddle and shifted herself for comfort.

She looked elegant and absolutely in control as she steered Fonteyn round to the rider's enclosure that led to the main competition ring.

Listening to Samantha Weston's progress, the crowd cheering every cleared fence, Ashton leaned over her mount's neck and stroked her glossy coat firmly.

"Let's show them what we're made of," Ashton whispered just loud enough for the mare to hear. "You're ready for this, and so am I – now let's go do it!"

Concentrating only on the ride ahead, Ashton didn't return the smile that Samantha gave her as she exited the ring – she didn't see or hear anything, the course was Ashton's only focus.

The announcer let the crowd know who was riding next and a cheer went up for Ashton, a popular local girl.

Wesley and I watched Ashton and Fonteyn as they lined up to begin the round against the clock.

"Shit! She's got that daredevil look on her face," I observed, not taking my eyes off my sister, and Wesley knew exactly the look I meant.

As they'd been growing up, Ashton had often gotten that look on her face, challenging Wes and her brothers to best her at something or other.

Once, he Chad and Matt had been swinging on a rope and then letting go to land in the river and Ashton had just had to have a go too.

She'd been 8 at the time – a scrawny little bitty thing who could have drowned in the fast flowing river – but she'd been determined to do everything the boys did and snuck onto the rope when they weren't looking.

"Get the hell off of there!" Chad had shouted when he'd realised what Ashton was doing. But she had only pushed harder with her skinny legs, working her way up higher as she stood on the large knot at the end of the rope.

Even then Wesley had liked her spirit, admired her daring and her spitting green eyes when she'd squared up to her big brother, telling Chad 'you're not the boss of me' and her mane of red hair making her look all the more fierce.

And Ashton had worked her way up to a good height on that rope, was swinging higher than any of the boys had before she'd let go and flown through the air after giving Chad a defiant glare.

Wesley held his breath as he watched her now, as daring as ever as she took the third fence then rounded quickly to line up the wall. Fonteyn didn't falter; horse and rider were moving as one, and then his breath eased out as they cleared the wall with inches to spare.

The breath he'd just allowed out was gasped back in as Ashton and Fonteyn took the turn to the water jump at breakneck speed cutting the corner alarmingly. But they took off cleanly, landed perfectly and swung round to take the double then took another hairpin turn to take the final triple.

The crowd went wild and Wesley and Matthias cheered just as loudly when the announcer gave Ashton's time of 41.5 seconds.

Moments later they watched as horse and rider rounded the horsebox looking very pleased with themselves.

"You maniac!" I berated her, but my grin told Ashton that I wasn't really angry. "I should use that crop to lash your arse," I persisted, but caught her to me in a proud brotherly hug when she slid out of the saddle to stand in front of me.

Looking over her brother's shoulder Ashton met Wesley's eyes and he gave her a nod looking every bit as proud of her as Matthias had.

"Miss Langdon..." an officious sounding voice spoke from just behind us and I let go of my sister to see who wanted her, "...I'm Clara Wentworth, director of the Equestrienne Youth Academy in Essex."

Taking the hand of the woman holding hers out towards her, Ashton frowned with some confusion. "I know of the academy, of course..." she began hesitantly, "...but why do you need to speak to me?"

"I go to a lot of these events..." the woman, who looked to be in her early thirties, began to explain, "...and I've seen you ride a number of times – you're good."

"Well...thank you," Ashton smiled, though her green eyes were still wary.

"You're very good," Clara Wentworth reiterated. "I want you to consider joining us." Then Clara reached out a hand to Fonteyn's neck and gave the mare a congratulatory pat, "As are you," she told the mare.

Feeling decidedly uncomfortable about this sudden turn of events, I stepped towards Ms Wentworth and gave her an assessing look. "You realise my sister is only 17..." I told her, "...I thought the academy only took 18-22 year olds."

"True...but I believe Ashton will be 18 in three months time — just right for the September intake," the woman smiled, then turned her gaze back to Ashton and raised an enquiring brow.

Turning to me, Ashton said, "I...what about the farm...the stables...?" Ashton wanted to say yes, but she had responsibilities she knew she couldn't just walk away from. "I've built up a good number of students in the riding school — who'll take the lessons if I go...you can't do everything?"

It's been hard on me since our older brother, Chad, had taken off. But I wouldn't stand in my sister's way, not when she was being given such an outstanding opportunity.

"Don't give that another thought..." I told Ashton with a grin, "...you're not indispensible. Pam can handle most of the riding lessons; I can take the ones she can't. And Mac has been telling me that his son is out of work — he can start any time so there really is no reason for you to turn down a place at the academy...unless it really isn't what you want?"

With all eyes on her, Ashton turned hers to Wesley.

Would he even care if she wasn't around anymore – she didn't think so? He's always with some bimbo or other and he's never shown an interest in her since *that* day.

"What are the costs involved?" Ashton turned back to Clara Wentworth, her mind back on the business in hand. "We can't afford some fancy academy and my brother is going to have to take on another farm hand if I go?"

"The academy is fully funded – we have private backers who are in the higher echelons of the equestrian society who want to nurture our talented youth to maintain our standing in the international arena," Clara explained proudly.

"You, and your horse, will reside at the academy and receive lessons from acclaimed instructors who will put you both through your paces," she told Ashton, her expression completely business like. "You will be entered into various events, some of those on the international circuit, and your progress monitored closely. If you do not continue to display the promise you have thus far shown, you will be let go." Clara looked directly into Ashton's eyes to bring this point home. "Only those who give 100% of their time and dedication will remain at the academy."

Meeting the older woman's challenging gaze head on, Ashton could hear the shocked gasps going on around her but determined to ignore them.

"You're on! I don't start anything I can't finish and I won't be the one who gets sent home!"

The last two riders had completed their jump off rounds and all the jump off riders were being called back into the ring.

"I look forward to seeing you in September..." Clara Wentworth held her hand out to Ashton and felt the younger woman's firm grip as she took it, "...now go and pick up your trophy – you just won."

CHAPTER THREE

Sitting with my head down over the farm accounts in what used to be Chad's study, I yawned loudly and took another gulp of black coffee.

Ok, I think I'm finally getting to grips with all this, but I'm going to need to take on more help and I'm not sure the finances can take it.

The riding school is doing well — so well that Pam is struggling to manage all the lessons on her own, and the stud side of things is building nicely — but the farm itself...well...

Jackson is working out well — Mac was right, his son is a natural with farm work. He looks at what needs doing and just gets right on in there and does it — exactly what we need - I just wish there was another one at home just like him!

Mac has made the barn into great living quarters – the two of them seem to get along great. And it helps with the wages – they get to live there rent free as part of their pay and it hasn't cost me much to extend the utilities to the barn.

"Hi, Matt, can I have a word?" Pam stood by the study door looking nervous.

"I was just thinking about you..." I smiled and waved a hand towards the chair next to my desk, "...I can't thank you enough for all your hard work, Pam. I know the riding school is booming and you need some help – I'm just trying to work out the finances to make that possible."

"Well, yes..." Pam began hesitantly, "...I've managed to arrange the lessons into manageable groups, but I've been getting more requests for private lessons – you know, one-to-ones, and that can be a lucrative side of the business, but I just can't do them on top of the group lessons," she explained sadly.

"Jesus. I wish Chad would hurry up and get over his love spat with Fallon, we could use his help about now," I confessed, pushing both hands back through my dark chestnut hair.

"And, Matt..." Pam continued, a grimace screwing up her pretty blue eyes, "...I need to tell you something that isn't good news." She hesitated but then dived in and delivered a resounding blow to my gut, "I've been offered another job — one of the mothers who brings her daughter to the riding school thought I would be ideal as a personal trainer and stable manager."

Slumping back in my seat, I stared at her open mouthed, then snapped my jaw shut and nodded resignedly. "No doubt that would mean a considerable raise in salary..." I guessed, and received a confirmatory nod. "I wish I could match it, but things are too tight at the minute," I admitted on a long troubled sigh. "But if you stay with us, I can promise that I'll make sure you get a sizeable bonus, and a raise, just as soon as I can manage it. In the meantime, I'll get on with hiring you some help — things can't continue the way they are."

Nodding, Pam looked at the man she'd had a crush on since her early teens and knew she wouldn't be going anywhere. How could she leave him in his time of need — how could she leave him, period!

"Thanks, Matt — the help will be much appreciated and will pay for itself by enabling me to do a few of those private lessons I was talking about," Pam smiled beautifully. "I might even be able to put together a mini competition — the entrance fees alone make that a worthwhile proposition and we can buy a decent cup for the winner out of the advance proceeds."

"Then you're staying...?" I gasped, unable to keep the astonishment and joy out of my voice and jumped to my feet at the same time.

Standing to get back to work, Pam gave Matt her best smile, thrilled to have made him so happy. "Looks like it, boss. I'd better get back at it; I have a group lesson due in half an hour and jobs to do before that."

"Pam...you're the best," I told her, then impulsively pulled her in for a hug and a firm, but brief, kiss on her lips. When she looked blankly up at me, I wasn't sure if I'd crossed a line and quickly apologised. "Sorry...sorry, just got carried away," and I stepped back abruptly, coughing to hide my embarrassment.

"Ok...well...I'll just get on...then," Pam smiled tentatively, then hurried from the room.

"Shit! What the hell made you do that?!" I sat down heavily in my seat and put my head in my hands.

Now she'll go running for the hills, or the new job, thanks to you grabbing at her that way. You idiot!

But far from running for the hills, Pam was smiling brighter than ever and had a new spring in her step.

He was just glad that I'm staying, she told herself, trying to be calm and rational. *But it felt soooo good... I just wish he'd noticed me before I threatened to leave — though he should have known it was an empty threat; I can't imagine leaving Langdon Farm, or Matthias.*

"You look happy..." Mac told her as he walked out of the tack room, "...you get a raise?"

He was so near the mark it made Pam laugh hilariously and brought Mac's son out of a nearby stable to see what was going on.

"Share the joke, I could use a good laugh," Jackson smiled broadly as he moved further into the stable yard.

"Actually, no raise..." she told them, hauling in a breath to calm herself, "...in fact, I just turned down a better paying job to stay working here – I couldn't leave Matt in the lurch like that."

Jackson frowned and scratched his head, "Soooo all this hilarity is really hysterics – you having lost your mind, that is," he chuckled softly.

"I suppose I must have," she grinned, then turned and walked away, a very definite spring in her step, to get ready for the imminent arrival of her riding students.

But Mac and Jackson stood looking after her, their heads now close together. "I don't know about losing her head..." Mac whispered conspiratorially, "...I'd say it's her heart that just got dropped at the boss' feet."

"You think?" Jackson frowned at his dad, then turned to watch Pam's progress. "Well, good luck to her – she'll need it if she's going up against Ms La-de-da Swain."

Returning his son's frown, Mac felt a groan of pity in his belly – he liked Pam, thought she was a good sort and would make an excellent farmer's wife, now he'd come to think about it. "How do you know Fenella Swain is in the picture – it's probably just village gossip – you know what Dersley Dale is like, full of bored people with nothing better to do than make up gossip just to pass the time!"

But Jackson was already shaking his head. "Not this time, pops – I've seen her myself, the way she drapes herself all over him at the slightest opportunity – and Ms Swain gets what Ms Swain wants, you know that!"

"Well, not this time..." Mac nodded firmly, "...not if I'm any judge of character. Matt Langdon is a good man, the only reason to marry the likes of Fenella Swain would be her daddy's money and I don't see the boss lowering himself to that sorry level!"

"Not even to save the farm he loves?" Jackson asked with a cocked brow. "It's been in his family for generations; I'd think he'd do pretty much anything not to lose it."

But Mac wouldn't hear of such talk, "I'm telling you, Matt would never sell himself so cheap – not even for the farm! He'll find a way through – this is a hard time for most farmers and Matt loves this place. It's in his blood..." Mac stated firmly, "...it's the very heart that beats in his chest."

"Exactly!" Jackson gave his father a telling look then returned to his work in the stables.

Feeling saddened by his son's comments, Mac tried to shrug them off as he rubbed saddle soap into a saddle that he'd got slung over a rail.

Damn it all to hell – the lad works more hours than his father or Chad ever did, he deserves a better break than the one he's getting right now. And it's not like it's down to poor management – the lad's doing the best he can in a rough economic climate – he's got people owing him money left, right and centre, as well as having bills of his own to settle. It just ain't right!

If Matt could read Mac's thoughts he would certainly have agreed with them. He was back pawing over the books, robbing Peter to pay Paul and managing, just, to make ends meet.

"Ok, looks like I've freed up enough to pay a stable hand basic money," I told myself, pleased to have juggled that much. *A few cut backs here and there and we'll manage until we get some money in at the end of the month. Things should get quite a bit easier then.*

Fenella Swain was throwing a tantrum that would rival any of the kids in the local nursery school.

"We need to throw a party!" she demanded of her harried father. "I want to invite Matthias Langdon over and that would be an ideal way for me to do it!"

"Couldn't you just invite him over for dinner?" Theodore Swain tried to mollify his irate daughter. "I mean, do we really need to invite half the village just so you can get cosy with Matt Langdon?"

"Well, of course we do," Fenella stared at her father as if he'd gone mad. "I don't want every nosy biddy knowing that I'm making a play for him – that would be-"

"The truth," her father put in with a smile.

"Embarrassing!" Fenella stomped her foot angrily.

"Alright, princess..." her father finally conceded, "...anything for you, baby." And he meant it, he adored his only child and would indulge her whims whenever they weren't too extreme. "But you can get your head together with Molly – I am not getting involved in getting a damned barn-party organised – I just pay the bills around here!"

"Fine," Fenella agreed, flouncing out of the sitting room to hunt down their housekeeper. Molly had organised lots of these events before, and at short notice as they nearly always took place on a whim of Fenella's.

Before the month was out, Molly March – an unfortunate name for so nice a person – had everything in order, even managing to get the invitations sent out first class. And, at Fenella's insistence, included first class stamped addressed envelopes to ensure speedy replies -

though Fenella had insisted on taking Matthias's invitation over herself.

"Well, why shouldn't I take the opportunity to go and see him..." she insisted when her father told Fenella that it might come across as 'pushy', "...it's not like we have regular meeting places in this damned village – unless you like the local pub!"

"Which Matt does," Molly commented distractedly while walking past them into the kitchen.

"What?!"

"Oh, I'm so sorry, I didn't mean to listen," Molly blushed wildly, then turned to scuttle quickly away.

"Molly, will you stop running away and tell me exactly what you meant?" Fenella demanded sharply.

The young housekeeper had only been in her job for six months and felt sure she was going to be for the chop. "I'm so sorry, miss – I really-"

"Molly!" Fenella cut off the housekeeper's apology and stood frowning down at her with hands on hips. "I don't care about all that, just tell me what you meant about Matt – does he frequent the local pub – and, if he does, who does he go with?"

Better not be with a woman or I'll scratch the bitch's eyes out!

"Well, I know he used to go in the Rose & Crown with

his brother and Wesley till Chad left and now it's just Matt and Wes," Molly babbled all at once, then hauled in a breath and let it out on a long sigh.

"So, he doesn't take girlfriends in there?" Fenella asked just to be sure.

"No, miss, not lately anyway," Molly replied, happier now that she seemed not to be the focus of attention.

"Not lately?!" Fenella barked out, making the housekeeper hunch her shoulders again. "Who was she and when were they last in there?"

"I.I don't remember when, miss, but it was Camille Parsons, the last I knew," Molly recalled, trembling under Fenella's angry gaze.

"Bloody hell! She's my best friend and she never even mentioned it," Fenella turned to her father, completely forgetting about Molly, who took the oportunity to escape. "Cam knows how much I like Matt – the bloody bitch must have gone behind my back!"

"Now, now..." Theodore Swain tried to placate his daughter, "...I'm sure Camille did no such thing. You heard Molly, it was a while ago since Matt was seeing her; it was probably all over even before you took a liking to the lad."

Bottom lip trembling, Fenella appeared undecided as to despair or another tantrum, but finally flung herself into her father's arms. "Oh, daddy, I like him s.sooooo much – I can't bear the thought of him with s.someone else."

"Then you'd better get your skates on..." Theo warned, "...there aren't many eligible young men in these parts, he won't stay available for much longer."

"Yes, you're right, as usual," Fenella smiled up adoringly at her father. "And you'll help me, won't you daddy? I mean, you do want me to be happy, don't you?"

"Let's see what the party brings, shall we?" he smiled and patted her back indulgently. "You may not need my help – you're a very eligable young woman and a damned beautiful one, if I'm any judge – and I rather think that I am!"

"Well, I do try my best," Fenella fingered her long blonde hair. "Now do stop distracting me, I must take Matt his invitation."

Chuckling to himself, Theo watched his daughter take off in a mad rush and just hoped to high heaven that she wouldn't get her heart broken.

Fenella's Porsche was white with two shapely thin stripes of blush pink along the sides. The interior was leather, also custom made in a matching pink, and Fenella looked like a barbie-doll on her way to Ken's house, driving with the top down.

With no one there to greet her, Fenella slammed the

door of her car to attract someone's attention, but got no joy.

Looking out over one of the fields, she could see a tractor at work but didn't think Matt was driving it.

Giving a good knock on the front door Fenella waited, none too patiently, for someone to answer it but again got no joy. "Oh this is ridiculous!"

Walking round the side of the house, Fenella made her way to the stable yard, calling out for Matt.

"Hey, what are you doing here?" I grinned, coming out of a stable that I was in the middle of mucking out. "Anything I can do for you?"

"It's more what I can do for you," Fenella grinned brightly, quite mollified now that she had found her man. "I wanted to make sure you got this," she said, and handed me an invitation.

"Hmm, very mysterious," and I took the white envelope opening it carefully. "Oh great, a barn dance," I grinned over the card at her. "What's it for this time – you seem to find umpteen excuses for hosting a good shin-dig."

But Fenella just shook her head, sending her fine blonde hair shimmering in the sunshine. "No excuses – not this time. I'm bored and I want to enjoy a party with my friends – isn't that excuse enough?" she laughed happily.

"You won't get an argument from me," I told her. "Have you invited Wes?"

"Of course – I know you two are joined at the hip," and Fenella rolled her eyes at me. "I just hope he brings one of his more 'educated' bimbos," and she rolled her eyes again.

"Oh, so this is for me and a friend?" I raised a quizzical brow at Fenella.

"It is..." she hesitated, then decided to throw caution to the wind, "...but I was hoping you would escort me."

I had instantly thought of inviting Pam, but I could hardly refuse to escort Fenella now.

"It would be my pleasure," I smiled, giving her a slight nod of my head.

"Oh that's marvellous! We'll have a ball, just you wait and see," she expounded, almost flinging her arms about his neck until she realised that Matt was covered in horse shit and hay and giggled to hide her embarrassment.

"I'm sure everyone will have a great time," I assured her, finding it odd how unsure of herself Fenella appeared to be. "You've never failed to throw a good party."

"Oh, thank you. Thank you, Matt, that really means a lot," Fenella smiled; not her usual uber confident smile but this time it felt genuine and heartfelt, knocking me a bit off balance.

"My pleasure. I'll see you there then," I told her, returning Fenella's smile and wondering what she was up to. Then I felt bad for my suspicious mind and asked, "What time would you like me to arrive – if I'm to be your escort I imagine you'll want me there before the guests start arriving?"

Lighting up like a Christmas tree, Fenella looked truly beautiful and again I felt like my world had tilted sideways.

"How thoughtful – thank you," Fenella smiled shyly. "If you could arrive around 7 the guests should start arriving around 7:30."

"Right you are, 7 it is," and I tipped an imaginary hat towards her.

Watching Fenella leave the yard in her short summer dress and stiletto heels, I had the feeling that more had just happened than me accepting a party invitation, but I had no clue what.

CHAPTER FOUR

"So, Fenella is giving one of her famous parties," Pam stated rather than asked, and forced a smile to lighten her words. "Sorry, couldn't help overhearing," she added when I raised a brow.

"I had thought of inviting you..." I told her, not realising that I'd sent Pam's heart racing, "...but as you no doubt heard, Fenella rather cornered me into being her escort. I'm still not sure I didn't miss something in that conversation," I mused, picking up the rake I'd been using prior to Fenella's visit.

Pam could have told me exactly what I'd missed — she'd picked up on Fenella's proprietary tone the moment she'd opened her pretty mouth.

Sodding rich girl! How's a girl like me supposed to compete with someone like her!

With Pam taking her frustration out on the work, I had to scoot aside when a fork full of horse dung flew at my feet. But I didn't say anything – just watched out of the corner of my eyes as Pam huffed loudly, having seemingly found something to be angry about.

Women! I'll never understand them if I live to be a 100! What the hell did I do to upset her – I told her I wanted to take her, didn't I? And she said she'd heard my conversation with Fenella, didn't she?

When a nob of dung flies past my ears I decided to cut and run. "Just going to make sure Mac's alright," I told Pam, before making a quick exit and crossing the yard to vanish into the tack room.

"Bloody, bloody, bloody man!" Pam seethed quietly, watching Matt go, and didn't feel any better for him leaving. Then Ronan gave his stall a good kick, vying for attention and no doubt wanting out. "And you can shut up too! I'm in no mood for males of any kind – got it!"

But after finishing the mucking out, Pam went to Ronan and gave his forehead a rub. "Alright, big boy, I'll get your bridle and let you out in the paddock for the rest of today – but no pulling, or you go straight back in your stall!"

Going to the tack room, Pam got Ronan's bridle and then decided to do some training with him, so took the lunge roller and rein and the running martingale to add to his bridle.

Training with the martingale on wasn't one of Ronan's favourite pasttimes, but he was getting much more manageable now that he was getting used to wearing it.

"That's it, boy, just take your time and let me do this up properly – we don't want any accidents," Pam warned the big Arabian horse who, for once, was standing more or less patiently. "Not in your nature to be obliging is it Ronan. But I guess that goes with the male gender of most species," Pam frowned as she attached the lunging rein to Ronan's bridle to make it easier to lead him out to the rear paddock.

The first time she'd done this, Matt had been with her with Mac and Jackson standing nearby just in case. And Ronan had been a handful alright; he'd reared up and flared his nostrils angrily the first time he'd worn the running martingale. But with Matt's help, and the security of knowing that she had the help of two more burly men if she needed them, Pam had won Ronan over. *After a fashion, anyway!*

"At least this way you get to go out in the field and get some exercise," she told the large stallion. "And now that you're mostly manageable, you even get to have some nookie – your stud services are highly sought after."

And as if in answer, Ronan gave a deep snort in a haughty 'what-else-would-you-expect' kind of a way.

Chuckling to herself, Pam ran a hand over his neck and gave him a gentle pat. "If I didn't know better, I'd think you understood every word I just said," and she gave him an assessing look out of the corner of her hazel eyes.

Ronan let out another snort and Pam let out a giggle. "That's a lovely sound and no mistake," I told her as I came alongside them. "Don't you usually get Mac or Jackson to walk with you and Ronan if I'm not around?"

"I did, at first," Pam corrected. "But he's been so good lately, I stopped asking them," and she gave me the same kind of sidelong look that she had not long before given Ronan. "They have enough to do – and besides, Ronan is getting much better since he got used to the martingale."

"Hmm, took a while, and I still don't know that I trust him completely – just look at his nostrils..." I warned, "...you can see the spirit rising in him – so don't you try to ride him...ever...is that clear?"

Bristling at what Pam saw as my high-handed attitude, her back naturally stiffened.

Boss or no boss, Pam wasn't a bloody novice to be spoken to like that! "I have been riding for a lot of years, Matthias Langdon..." and I knew I was in trouble when she used my full name, "...so I know whether or not I can handle a horse and I prize my life more than the thrill that riding Ronan would give me!"

Having opened the paddock gate for her, I stood back while Pam led Ronan past me.

"Just making sure that point was understood," I replied cautiously, watching as Pam moved the lunging rein from the bridle to the lunge roller around Ronan's midrif. "I told you what happened to Ashton that time – if it hadn't been for Wes she could have been a goner."

But Pam merely cocked a brow at me, then returned to the business of checking Ronan's tack for a proper fit.

"I have been riding for as many years as Ashton was old, at that time at least," Pam reminded me. "Plus I have more sense than to go off on Ronan alone. If I were to ever ride him-" And she broke off to frown over at me as I made to interrupt her. "I didn't say I was going to – I just said 'if' I were going to; then I'd make sure I was with someone like you or Wes on a horse that could keep up with Ronan if he did try to bolt for it. I'm not a complete idiot!"

"Fine. Fine. Just as long as that's understood," and I watched as Pam turned a very stiff back on me and continued to work with Ronan.

Our relationship has never been one of the usual boss and employee variety – we've known each other since we were kids. *She's seen me starkers, for christ sake – though we were around 3 at the time, according to my mother.*

It had been a really hot summer and all us kids had apparently been running around in the buff while dad sprayed water over us with the hosepipe. A childhood spent on Langdon Farm was certainly hard work but also fun.

Watching Pam's shapely figure move gracefully in her tight fitting jodhpurs, I found myself getting more than a tad uncomfortable in my jeans.

"I'll see you later, if you're sure your ok...?"

In answer, Pam raised a hand to wave me off and didn't even bother to turn her head in my direction.

"Women!" I exclaimed, then smiled in my usual happy-go-lucky way. "Can't live with them but I wouldn't want to live without them!" And I couldn't help chuckling to myself as I got back to work on the farm.

Although our relationship was more friends than boss and employee I had, so far, been reluctant to make a move on Pam because I didn't want to ruin our friendship. But love, or lust, sometimes takes on a life of it's own and I was finding it more and more difficult to keep my hands off of my stable manager.

The day of Fenella's party dawned bright and sunny and matched my upbeat mood.

It was almost the end of the month and some of my biggest outstanding debtors had promised to pay their accounts in a few days time. *And just in time, too. There's virtually nothing in Peter's coffers to pay Paul any more!*

Pam had been right about taking on a new stable hand paying for itself – the increase in private riding lessons had increased just as she predicted.

"Hey, Lizzy, how's it going?" I smiled over at the young girl who worked Saturday mornings as part of her working week.

"It's going great, Mr Langdon," Lizzy smiled happily.

"Good, I'll give Ronan his feed then let him out in the paddock after I've groomed him, then you can muck out his stall," I told her, impressed by the girl's willingness to learn and work hard.

I started Lizzy on minimum wages, but if she kept up the good work I'd put her money up at the end of the month when the farm finally got some money in from our late payers.

"Here you go, boy." I put a bucket of feed in front of Ronan before getting to work with a curry comb. Funnily enough, the big stallion had always enjoyed being groomed. *I suppose it must be soothing.*

"Ok, looking good." I patted Ronan's neck then swapped the curry comb for a dandy brush and knew that the horse really enjoyed a good brushing. Putting my back into it, I got to work on Ronan's shoulder and flank. Putting a hand on his rump to let the horse know that I was moving round to do the other side, I finished off the grooming process.

"Are you gonna let me look at your feet today?" I asked Ronan, who kept right on eating his oat mix. "Sure, Matt, help yourself," I answered myself with a low chuckle, and reached for the hoof pick to clean out Ronan's hooves.

"You know, talking to a horse could constitute talking to yourself..." Lizzy grinned from the doorway, watching as I got the large horse to lift each foot and let me work on it, "...and you know what they say that's a sign of." Her grin widened when I gave her a sideways look and rolled my eyes.

In just two weeks Lizzy had gone from being so shy that she barely uttered a word, to being relaxed enough to have the odd joke with me. She was still wary of strangers, but the farm hands seemed to have taken her under their wing and Lizzy was beginning to blossom.

"Are you waiting to get in here?" I asked her when Lizzy continued to stand by the stable doors.

"Yep, I've done the rest of the mucking out and put fresh hay nets in for them," Lizzy explained. "Ronan's is the last one – then I'm going to work in the tack room, unless you have other jobs you'd rather I do?"

"No, that's sounds fine...we'll be out of your way in just a mo." And I closed and locked the stall door while I crossed to the tack room to get Ronan's bridle.

"Ok, boy, you can have a rest from the martingale and enjoy a good run," I told the horse, and gave him a gentle pat on the side of his neck.

"He looks so beautiful after he's been groomed," Lizzy observed, looking adoringly at the very regal stallion.

"Hmm...just don't let him fool you – Ronan is a real handful, you never go into his stall or the paddock when he's around – ok?"

"Pam's already warned me lots of times," Lizzy smiled. "But I still think he's a handsome brute – do you ever ride him?"

"Not willingly, though I have done," I grimaced at the memory. "I usually manage to talk Wes into giving him some exercise – he's used to willful animals and seems as expert at riding Ronan as Chad was."

Lizzy frowned curiously. "Who are they – Wes and Chad – are they your brothers?"

"Chad is, and Wes is as good as – we all grew up together and generally got the same smacks across our behinds for getting into trouble," I chuckled then, and led Ronan out of his stall.

Walking like a gentleman, Ronan could have been mistaken for a good natured horse that anyone could ride, until they got on his back.

Walking along side me, Lizzy look up at Ronan in awe. "He's very tall – how many hands is he?"

"17," I told her, and asked Lizzy to open the paddock gate then go back out and lock it behind her. I detached the lead rein from the bridle and gave the horse a pat to let him know he was free to go. But Ronan didn't need any encouragement, he took off across the enclosed field, his tail thrashing and his mane flying.

Climbing the paddock fence, I heaved myself over it and came to stand beside Lizzy. "When you've mucked out Ronan's stall and done whatever needs doing in the tack room, you can get off home."

"But I've still got a couple more hours to do – the mucking out will only take about 20 minutes and there's only a small amount of tack that needs cleaning," she confessed, worried that I might think she was shirking her duties.

"Fine. You've worked hard and got the jobs done – or will have by the time you get off," I smiled down at her. "We don't clock in and out around here – when you've finished the work get off home."

CHAPTER FIVE

When I pulled up at the side of the large Swain residence, I had to admire Fenella's ability to make a splash.

There were lights in the trees leading up to the house and across to the nearby barn, and all would become more dazzling as the evening progressed. Even the barn itself had been given a facelift with bunting draped all over it.

Chuckling at the sign tied to the front of the barn with the colourful bunting, I had to admire Fenella's simple, straight to the point approach to life.

Good Lord! That's a typical Fenella touch! 'Live life, have fun and be happy – Let's Party!'

"Your father is way too indulgent," I told Fenella as she came down the front steps of the main house to greet me. "And you look...well...you look amazing, actually."

In a very slinky midnight blue mini-dress and barely-there silver sandals, Fenella came to a halt on the bottom step, standing eye to eye with me, a delightful smile spreading across her pretty face.

"That reaction makes all the effort I took worthwhile..." she said, her voice low and sultry, "...and deserves to be rewarded."

A hand reached around the back of my neck and slid long fingers through my hair before pulling me gently forward. In slow motion, her lips took possession of mine and my brain went into a mindless whirl.

"Wow..." I smiled dazedly, "...you taste every bit as good as you look!"

Fenella's smile turned smug as she looked over my shoulder to see who was arriving.

"Looks like Carl Rutterman's car," she informed me, and I turned to look in the direction of the new arrival.

"Bit early, isn't he?" I watched the swanky Range Rover continue its journey then pull up next to my car at the side of the house.

"Evening..." Rutterman bellowed at the top of his voice, "...are we the first to arrive?" And he strode towards Fenella and I, leaving a-none-too-pleased looking young woman to follow in his wake.

When the young woman caught up she glared at Rutterman with blood in her eyes. "The next time you invite me to a party have the decency to show some manners!" Then she adjusted her stance and continued to glare, "No, scratch that, there won't be a next time!"

"Oh do stop whinging, Patty," Rutterman told her, then grabbed Patty round the waist to pull her into a rough embrace. "We're here to party — try to enjoy yourself, there's a good girl," and, ignoring the fire in his companion's eyes, Rutterman dipped his head to kiss her.

I honestly didn't see it coming — Patty twisted in the big man's arms and brought her knee up between his legs. Cringing, I let out a groan of sympathy as Rutterman crumpled to the ground and Patty stood, hands on hips, with a very satisfied smile on her face.

"Er, perhaps you'd better take Patty inside," I suggested, looking at Fenella for help in preventing the situation from escalating any further.

"My pleasure," Fenella chuckled. "Come on, Patty, I'll get you a drink — you deserve one. Rutterman's been asking for that for a very long time!"

"Bloody hell," Rutterman groaned, hands between his legs clasping his wedding tackle and praying it would still function properly. "Damned woman...don't know why I bothered asking her...not all that many options though in this neck of the woods."

"Hmm…" I reached down to help Rutterman up, "…that's because you've already offended all the decent ones and they wouldn't touch you with a barge-pole!"

Surprising me, Rutterman let out a raucous laugh. "Don't know what all the fuss is about – I give 'em a good time, don't I? Even wine and dine 'em before getting 'em between the sheets."

And I could see right then, Rutterman really didn't think there was anything wrong with his brash manner.

"Come on, let's get you a drink," I suggested, helping the big man to make his way up the front steps.

When we walked into the sitting room, the two girls were talking and laughing together, giving us the merest glance as we walked into the room.

"Still in the dog-house then," Rutterman huffed.

I couldn't say that I blamed Patty for her reaction – Rutterman really could be an unthinking dolt sometimes.

"Do you want to take a seat and I'll fetch you a drink?" I offered, sympathising with the other man's grimace.

"Not really, old chap…" Rutterman looked at a chair with fear in his eyes, "…don't think sitting on me balls will help 'em recover – if you see what I mean."

Oh yes, I did understand completely. Not that I'd ever had a woman do that to me, but I'd been caught in the balls by the wayward hoof of one of the dairy cows when

I'd been a young teenager, and I'd never forgotten the pain of it.

Bloody eye-watering – couldn't sit down comfortably for a week!

Walking over to where the women were standing, I was just about to ask Rutterman what he would like when the man himself spoke up.

"This it then?" Rutterman looked askance at the few drinks bottles set out on the top of a lovely mahogany cabinet.

"No, dunderbrain!" Fenella rolled her eyes at the big man now standing at her side. "It's called a 'barn party' for a reason – all the food and drinks are in the barn. If you hadn't turned up so early we'd have greeted you there!"

But if Fenella thought to make Rutterman squirm she failed entirely.

"Ah. Right-ho. In that case, make mine a whiskey. A double," he added, casting a frown Patty's way. "Medicinal, you know."

Pouring his drink, Fenella handed him a glass with a generous measure of amber liquid in it. "Want anything in that?" she asked with a quirked brow.

"Not on your life!" Rutterman barked gruffly. "You don't mess with perfection, young woman!"

"You really are an arrogant shit," Fenella told him with a resigned sigh. "I am only two years younger than you yet you talk like you're Methuselah!"

"Not so much to do with age..." and Rutterman tapped the side of his nose knowledgeably, "...as what you know and your life experiences. There isn't much I haven't seen or done!"

The two women looked at each other and shook their heads in despair.

"Was that another car I just heard?" Fenella asked, crossing to the sitting room window to check.

I had crossed the room with her and raised a brow at the convoy of cars winding its way down the long drive. "Looks like the rest of your guests arranged to come together. Crikey, Fenella, how many people did you invite?"

"I don't really know – I just made up a list of all my friends and neighbours around our age and Molly sent out the invites," she explained nonchalantly. "Come on, let's go out to the barn and get this party started!"

"Hell's teeth, Fenella, you've even got a live band," I exclaimed when we entered the barn so as to greet the arriving guests.

"This barn is so big it needs a good sound system to fill it adequately," Fenella told him, then let out a little squeal of delight when one of her best friends entered the barn.

From that moment on I felt like I was on show – Fenella never actually put it into specific words, but the impression she was giving was one of us being a 'couple', and I wasn't sure I was comfortable with that idea.

Pam knows some of these people – what if it gets back to her that I'm hooked up with Fenella? Hell, I know we're not exactly dating ourselves, but I still feel like I'm being unfaithful. Which is bloody stupid, come to think of it!

"What's wrong, sweetie?" Fenella frowned up at me with genuine concern in her baby blue eyes.

Seeing it, I felt guilty that I'd been thinking of Pam. *Christ, women are so damned complicated!*

"Not a thing," I stated, almost convincing myself that it was the truth. "Come on, let's dance, I like this number."

The band was terrific; in fact, I thought I actually recognised some of the band members from the telly, which wouldn't have surprised me in the least as Fenella's father was rich as hell and totally over the top when it came to his daughter's happiness.

What Fenella wants Fenella gets and just now she seems to want me! Well, I'm hers for the evening and then I'll just disentangle myself as delicately as I can.

The night passed quickly, everyone enjoying

themselves and dancing to the band that I now knew had a current top 10 hit in the pop charts.

Extricating myself from Fenella's clutches had been even more difficult than I'd imagined.

Hell, I only signed up to be her escort not her partner for life! The way Fenella took on you'd think I broke off an official engagement

Pam couldn't understand why Matt was so distracted. She'd tried to engage him in conversation about Fenella's party but he'd shrugged it off and looked troubled.

Getting a fresh bale of straw for bedding, Pam set about mucking out some of the stables and tried not to think about Matt or what might have happened to upset him. But it was hard; she'd never seen him so preoccupied and worried that it might have something to do with the farm.

A little while later, Pam finished up in the stables then went to check on the tack ready for the riding lesson she had scheduled for that afternoon.

"Hi, Mac..." she greeted the farmhand, who was repairing some stitching on one of the saddles, "...isn't it a lovely day? We haven't had a summer like this for years."

"I don't think England has ever seen a summer like this," Mac replied, wiping his damp brow with a cloth from his pocket. "I swear I've lost half a stone in sweat this past week," he declared with a frown.

Chuckling, Pam took down one of the bridles and checked it was intact and ready for use, then moved on to another one.

"Getting ready for another lesson?" Mac asked, watching her progress.

"Yep – got six in this afternoon's group – good job we got that new pony last week," she smiled over at the man who was nodding in satisfaction at his handy-work.

"I was surprised Matt got a new horse, truth-be-known," Mac told her, and Pam turned to regard him curiously. "Well, we all know the farm is struggling – I didn't think he had any money over to go buying new horses is all I meant."

But Pam shook her head, turning to fully look at the concerned man as he lifted the mended saddle back in its place. "It wasn't like that – Matt took Daisy-belle in when her owner couldn't afford to keep her. He didn't buy her at all – it was either Matt took her or the knackers' yard would. Her owner did try to sell her but got no response, even when she finally put 'free to a good home'," Pam explained.

"Hmm, people just don't realise how much it costs to keep a horse properly," Mac nodded sagely. "But even if the boss didn't pay for the horse, he's still got to house and feed it, don't he?"

Frowning, Pam considered Mac and decided to ask him if he knew what was going on with Matt. "He was fine the last time I saw him, now he barely strings two words together no matter how much I try. I think something's wrong," Pam confided, her face betraying the depth of her worry.

"Now then, don't go fretting about Matt — he knows how to take care of himself and he's doing a fine job with the farm," Mac declared, more confidently than he actually felt. In truth, Mac had been fearing for his and Jackson's jobs for a week or two now. "The boss said he's waiting on some late payments that are due in any day — that's why I can't order any more feed for the dairy herd just yet."

"And then everything will be ok?" Pam asked hopefully.

"Far as I know," Mac smiled reassuringly.

Watching her leave the tack-room, Mac thought about what Pam had said about Matt and wondered if his boss' troubles were deeper than he'd let on.

Sitting with my head in my hands, I was contemplating just how deep the farm's financial troubles had become. I'd spent a lot of time on the phone trying to chase up the late payments that had been promised, only to be given the run around by all of them.

I never would have thought Hank Carter would have let me down – he knows how hard things have been for everyone in the farming community – and he'd promised payment by the end of the month, damn him!

Stiffening my resolve, I decided that the time had come to take some action and I went upstairs to change.

Looking in the long mirror in my bedroom, I straightened my tie and tugged it a little looser.

I hate these damned things but I suppose it will be worth it if I get the loan I'm about to ask for! It was good of Carl Morrison to see me at such short notice – but then he's been a friend of my dad's for years. Let's hope that's enough to convince him to lend me some money.

Parking in the bank's rear car park, I made my way to the front of the bank and gratefully walked through its doors to the air-conditioned interior.

Smiling at the enquiry desk receptionist, I put a finger between my neck and the collar of the shirt I was wearing, giving her a look that said 'it's bloody hot out there'.

"I'm here to see Mr Morrison – my name's Matthias Langdon," I informed her.

Picking up the phone in front of her, the receptionist let the bank manager know that his next appointment had arrived. Replacing the handset, she turned back to me and invited me to take a seat while I waited. "Would you like a glass of cold water?" she asked, registering my discomfort.

"That would be great," I smiled gratefully. "England is getting more like the tropics every day." *And this suit doesn't help matters!*

The cold water barely touched the sides as I gulped down the refreshing drink. "Thanks, that was just what I needed," I said, handing back the now empty glass.

Charmed and delighted by the handsome young man's smile, the receptionist almost floated back to her desk.

Minutes later she walked back over and told me, "Mr Morrison is ready for you now."

Knowing the way, I walked through a nearby door and along to the office at the end of a small corridor.

"Come in," Carl Morrison beckoned on hearing my knock. "Matt, how are you?" he smiled, standing to offer his hand across the desk in greeting.

"Personally I'm fine..." I smiled ruefully, "...but the farm is struggling."

"I'm sorry to hear that," Carl waved a hand towards a seat on the other side of his desk and waited while I made myself comfortable. "Does Charley know how bad things are?"

Charles Langdon is my father – he and my mother have retired from the farm and have taken off to travel for a while, making up for all the years they never took a holiday.

"Not his problem anymore," I shook my head, pursing my lips firmly. "I have a few late payers for beef and produce I've supplied – once they've settled up the farm will be fine; till then I have a cash-flow problem."

Smiling his understanding, Carl Morrison nodded his head and took out a pad and pencil. "Ok Matt, give me the bottom line and we'll see what we can do."

As I was about to lay the farm's finances open to Carl, the telephone rang and the bank manager grimaced an apology then took the call.

"Carl Morrison..." he stated, then listened as his secretary informed him who was on the line, "...I see, put him through."

In the second it took for the call to be transferred, Carl had stood and taken the mobile handset telling me that he would return in just a moment.

Looking idly round the smart office, I read a few framed certificates that Carl had hanging proudly on his wall.

Not bad – I didn't realise Carl had a degree. Would have thought he'd have aimed higher than a bank manager with all that learning behind him.

When Carl returned he looked flushed and a little

shaken as he retook his seat and seemed to find it difficult to meet my eyes. "I can't believe the timing of that call," he told me, his demeanour completely changed from the man who had greeted me with so much warmth.

"Something wrong?" I asked, a sudden knot of dread twisting in my gut.

"I'm afraid that was one of the top bosses at head office," Carl explained, picking up the pad and pencil and pushing them back into a draw. "Apparently our lending funds are frozen for new customers; I'm afraid I won't be able to help you after all."

Regarding Carl with narrowed eyes, I tried to consider my options calmly. "I've never asked the bank for help before..." I stated with pride, "...and I wouldn't be here now if there were any other course of action open to me. But Langdon farm is not a new customer — we've banked with Western Alliance since the bank was started here. Damn it man, my grandfathers banked with you for heaven's sake!"

"I realise that..." Carl Morrison shifted uncomfortably in his seat but didn't back down, "...but your family have never taken out a loan with the bank, that makes you a new customer as far as credit is concerned — I'm sorry, Matt."

"So, I'm being penalised for the fact that my family

has always worked hard to keep itself out of debt?!"

"I'm so sorry, Matthias..." Carl sighed heavily, holding his palms out in front of him in a helpless gesture, "...if there were any way round it..."

Shaking my head in disbelief, I stood and stared at the man whom my father had called friend for so many years. Moving to the door and opening it, I turned back to Carl and said, "Charley would be ashamed of you," then I stepped into the corridor, closing the door quietly behind me.

Walking out of the bank and into the street, I had to screw up my eyes to block the glare of a blazing sun.

Now what?!

<u>CHAPTER SIX</u>

With a heavy heart, I made my way back to my car and found Fenella standing by it.

Seeing my troubled face, Fenella's smile slipped and she stepped towards me cautiously. "What's wrong – you look awful," she exclaimed softly.

"Thanks," I replied with an unhappy shrug and made to walk past her to my car.

"Matt...?" Fenella turned, watching me open the car door and waited for me to look at her. "I saw your car and waited to apologise for my behaviour on Saturday – can't we at least be friends?"

Looking at Fenella it was like I'd only just realised she was there, but I managed to force a smile. "Sure...no worries."

Hands on hips, Fenella got angry, "Matthias Langdon,

don't you dare get behind the wheel of that car – you are in no fit state to drive!"

Bemused by her statement and severe demeanour, I just looked back at Fenella with a frown of confusion. "What the hell...?"

Walking up to me, Fenella shook her head on a sigh. "You look like a puppy dog that's been whipped to within an inch of its life – will you please tell me what's wrong!"

Rubbing a hand over my tired eyes, I leaned back against the car and found myself telling Fenella everything.

"I can't lose the farm," I finished sadly, the depth of my despondency openly apparent.

Wearing her heart on her sleeve, Fenella touched one hand to my arm and the other to my cheek. "Let me help you," she pleaded, watching the questions gather in my saddened eyes. "I'll talk to daddy this evening, tell him that I need some money for a shopping trip with Camille-"

"No!" I snapped, cutting Fenella off mid flow. "I am not taking money from you – and I am especially not taking it when you'd be lying to your own father!"

"So you'd rather keep your pride and lose your family's farm - is that it?" Fenella asked rolling her eyes.

"No..." I sighed, all pretence of pride gone as my shoulders slump heavily, "...but I won't let you lie to your father, ok."

"Ok, I get that," Fenella agreed, knowing that I had too many scruples to do anything underhanded. Not that Fenella saw it that way; her dad was always willing to give her all the money she ever wanted – she probably wouldn't even need to give him a reason so she wouldn't be lying to him anyway.

"So what are you going to do?" Fenella asked when I remained silent.

"I don't know. I haven't heard from Chad in quite a while and I definitely don't want to tell Ashton that the farm is in trouble – there's nothing she can do about it so why worry her," he explained when Fenella gave him a curious look.

"From what I hear, Ashton is doing really well on the show-jumping circuit – her winnings might be enough to tide you over for a while," Fenella suggested hopefully.

"Winnings?" I was surprised, then I laughed with astonishment, though mostly at my own idiocy in not realising that Ashton might actually earn a decent living doing the very thing she loves.

"I happen to know that one of the competitions Ashton won recently netted her prize money in the region of £25K," and Fenella cocked a brow at me. "There's a reason Clara Wentworth wanted her to join the academy – Ashton's damned good and there's word on the grapevine that Clara's grooming her for the Olympic team!"

"Wow!" I must have looked comical, all wide eyed and taken aback. "Then why hasn't Ashton said anything? You'd think she'd want the world and his dog to know how well she's doing."

"To be fair, Clara has only just allowed Ashton to start competing in the bigger competitions," Fenella admitted. "So, maybe she wants to make sure it isn't just beginners luck... and Ashton doesn't know anything about the Olympic thing – Clara wouldn't want her head to grow any bigger than it already is."

Now it was my turn to raise a brow, "Are you calling my little sister a bighead?"

Not sure if she'd upset him, Fenella hesitated then shrugged and said, "You damned well know she is. Be honest about it, Matt – Ashton thinks she's the best rider out there."

Chuckling softly, I had to agree. "Yes, she does doesn't she. But then, Ashton has always believed in herself and no one has, as yet, proved her wrong."

"Well, she won't win every competition she enters so little Ashton will have to learn to cope with defeat sometime," Fenella frowned up at Matt.

"True enough," I nodded, though my prideful smile

didn't slip. "I still don't want to bother her with farm business," I added stubbornly. "Ashton needs to have her mind on what she's trying to achieve – knowing the farm is sinking out from under me isn't going to do anything but distract her and maybe ruin her career before it's had a chance to begin."

Standing resolute, I pushed away from the car door and put a hand on Fenella's arm, "Thanks for listening, I'll manage somehow - we Langdon's always do."

With that he was gone and Fenella was no nearer to winning him over than she had been before.

I just know daddy would give me the money if I asked him – I also know Matt would never take it – so now what do I do? I can't let Matt lose the farm, it's in his blood, he'd be a broken man and I won't just stand by and watch that happen!

When I got back to the farm I was confronted by Mac and could see the man's concern in his eyes.

"What's going on, Mac?"

Scratching his wiry greying hair, Mac looked uncomfortable but determined. "Can we talk in the office, boss?" Mac asked, gruffly clearing his throat.

For a moment I just looked at the farmhand who has become a dear friend over the many years he has worked for my family, and then I gestured for Mac to follow me inside.

Once in the office I offered Mac a cup of coffee but he shook his head and said, "No thanks, boss."

Pouring myself a cup, I took it over to my desk and dropped into my seat, indicating that Mac should do the same.

"Ok, Mac, I've known you a lot of years and I've never seen that look on your face before – what is it, it has to be something bad," I guessed, and watched the farmhand nod gravely.

"I tried to order some feed this morning – we're almost completely out," Mac explained, then proceeded to clear his throat again, embarrassment seeming to make speech difficult. "We're out of credit, boss – I explained that we're all waiting on late payments, that it's a sign of the economic climate at this time, but they wouldn't listen and refused to make a delivery till the bill is paid up. I'm sorry, boss – I tried several others but they want cash in advance."

I frowned at that, "They actually said that?"

Nodding again, Mac shifted in his seat like it had grown hot and uncomfortable beneath him. "You know, my boy and I, we understand that times are hard..." Mac began, not quite looking me in the eyes, "...and we were reckoning up our savings-"

But I cut him off abruptly, moved unbelievably at what

I knew he was about to suggest but not willing to take Mac up on it. "No, Mac, I won't take your money – though I want you to pass on to Jackson that I'm gratified by the loyalty that both of you have shown. I do have another option..." I smiled ruefully and rubbed a hand over my tired eyes, "...it's just not one that I would ordinarily take if I weren't in such a tight corner."

Mac still looked uncomfortable but stayed sitting opposite the boss he respects greatly. "Then maybe you shouldn't ought to take it," Mac suggested quietly.

"Don't worry, I'm not going to sell the farm," I laughed derisively. "Though maybe it deserves a better manager than me – I really seem to have screwed things up since Chad left."

"That's stuff and nonsense," Mac surprised me and himself by voicing his opinion out loud. "I mean, it's the way of farming these days – they're all in the same boat and you'd think Macey would allow for that fact!"

My smile became less cynical as I regarded my outraged farm hand. "I don't suppose Macey can afford to wait for payment too long either," I sympathised. "As you rightly say, most of us farmers are in the same boat – Macey can't provide feed to everyone on never ending credit."

Mac didn't reply but made a gruff noise of dissent.

Standing, I walked around my desk to Mac who had also gotten to his feet. "Use what we've got – I'll go and do the necessary to get us the funds to keep us going."

Hesitating for just a moment, Mac nodded his head then left to carry out his boss' orders. But a feeling of unease was left in the older man's wake.

Theodore Swain was working in his office when he was told that Matthias Langdon was waiting to see him. "I've got to go – but you remember what I said, you give that boy one more penny of credit and I'll ruin you, and you know I can do it!"

Replacing the phone in its cradle, Fenella's father got up from his desk and went out to the hallway, crossing it to the lounge where Matt was waiting.

"Matt, how are you doing?" Theo greeted him with an outstretched hand and a broad smile.

Taking the hand held out to me, I shook it politely and just hoped that the older man didn't notice my sweaty palms. "Actually, the farm isn't doing so well," I admitted, and felt my stomach clench uncomfortably.

"I'm sorry to hear that," Theo replied sounding sincere. "Take a seat and tell me what I can do to help."

"Well, I went to the bank and asked for an overdraft or a loan..." I began to explain, not wanting Fenella's father to think that I was trying to take advantage of his daughter's connections, "...but they told me their policies have changed, that they are not allowed to extend credit to new borrowers." I sat up straighter, pride stiffening my spine, "Langdon farm has always managed its own finances in the past – we've never needed credit, but now it seems that has gone against us."

"You're not the only one," Theo consoled him. "I've heard tell of other farmers suffering the same way. The banks are all too quick to lend money in times of plenty, but in times of need they're only quick to foreclose on outstanding mortgages or loans. Damned money grabbers!"

"Well, thankfully we own the farm free and clear," I stated with some pride. "However, we still have to buy supplies and animal feed and we're scraping the barrel on both."

Getting to his feet, Theo looked down at me with what appeared to be fatherly concern. "Come with me, Matthias, – we'll talk this over in my office."

By the time I left the Swain house I had a large cheque in my pocket and a lead weight in my heart.

Going into town, I deposited the cheque before I had time to change my mind and tear it up. The terms of the loan were cruel and unusual, but I'd felt I had no choice but to agree to them.

I had no proof to back up the thoughts dancing around in my head as I returned to Langdon Farm, but I was pretty sure I now knew why no one had been willing to extend my credit.

Is there no limit to what the man won't do for his daughter?! I've never heard anything so outrageous, but what other choice did I have? And what if Fenella is behind all this – she's pretty relentless when she wants her own way – it really wouldn't surprise me!

Going back to my office I got on the phone to Macey, and my other suppliers, to get things moving again.

With an extremely heavy heart, I went out in search of Mac and Jackson to tell them the good news.

"I want to thank you both for your hard work and your loyalty," I began, looking from father to son. "But we'll be alright now – there's feed on the way and you don't need to worry about ordering more or getting supplies – I've sorted the finances and we're out of the red."

Mac didn't smile, he knew his boss had had to do something he really didn't want to in order to get them out of trouble, and had a feeling that his actions might come back to haunt them all.

"Have you seen Pam and Lizzy around?" I asked, preparing to walk to the stables.

"Pam's giving Lizzy a riding lesson in the back

paddock," Jackson supplied obligingly.

Giving them a wave, I turned and walked away to the stable yard.

For some reason that I wasn't sure of, I needed to see Pam. I not only felt horribly guilty for having made such a diabolical agreement with Theodore Swain, I was also feeling suddenly bereft.

Seeing that the stable yard was indeed empty and that Daisy-belle was missing from her stall, I made my way round to the back paddock.

Lizzy was smiling fit to burst as she walked Daisy-belle around the paddock, doing as Pam instructed with her feet.

"Heels down, Lizzy and just the toes of your feet through the stirrups," Pam told the young girl.

"Hey, Matt, see this," Lizzy grinned over as I climbed up to sit on the paddock fence and watch her progress.

"Looking good, Lizzy – how's it feel?"

"It's amazing, just how I thought it would be, and Pam says I have a natural seat," Lizzy declared proudly.

Turning her head to momentarily roll her eyes at me, Pam took in my smart suit and tie and the worried look on my face.

"That's enough for now, Lizzy," Pam told the new stable girl. "I'll help you down and then you can lead

Daisy-belle back to her stable and give her a rub down."

"Ok," Lizzy agreed reluctantly, but did as she was told without complaint. "Will you teach me again when we have time?" she asked eagerly, taking the gentle mare's reins and leading her towards the paddock gate.

"We should have time tomorrow morning before the group lessons," Pam nodded. "But you'll need to get your jobs done in a timely manner if we're to pull it in."

"Oh I will," Lizzy smiled adoringly at Pam.

Standing holding the paddock gate open for horse and groom to pass through, I waited for Pam to follow them.

"What's wrong?" she asked without preamble once Lizzy was out of earshot.

"Not a thing," I lied, my heart clenching at the sight of her. "I've just had a lot of financial business to tie up today, but everything should be fine from now on."

"You're sure," Pam stared up at him with uncertain eyes, willing her pessimism to be nothing more than worrywarting on her part.

"I'm sure – I went to the bank this morning, hence the suit and tie," I explained, but didn't fill her in on the rest of my morning's business.

A smile of relief came over Pam's face, lighting her eyes in just that way I have always liked.

"Well I'm glad to hear it..." Pam put a hand to his arm,

"...seems like you've been carrying the weight of the world around on your shoulders this last couple of months."

"No need to worry your pretty head anymore..." I smiled to hide my troubles, "...Matthias Langdon has it all under control."

CHAPTER SEVEN

The first time I asked Fenella Swain out on a date I almost confessed everything – the deal with her father and the fact that any relationship we may have was because of it.

She had been so excited, so genuinely pleased that I had finally asked her out. Fenella had gone all out on her appearance too – she'd gone out shopping with her good pal Camille and spent her daddy's money like it was water.

"You like?" she asked, doing a twirl in her parent's living room.

Oh yes, I'd liked alright. There was nothing not to like about Fenella. She had the body to go with the beautiful face and lush blonde hair, but she wasn't Pam.

I'd taken her to dinner at one of the few higher end

restaurants that Dersley Dale boasted and we'd eventually had a good time.

It had taken me a while just to feel comfortable among such wealth as the restaurant attracted – but I've never been ashamed of my farming roots and soon found myself enjoying Fenella's company.

The fact that I had enjoyed Fenella's company surprised me; I hadn't seen the funny, happy, chatty side of her before. So often I'd seen the spoiled brat that had a hissy fit if she didn't get what she wanted as soon as she wanted it and now, of course, she wanted me.

By the end of that night I had even managed to forget that I'd been forced into asking Fenella out and that had surprised me even more.

When I'd asked Fenella to join me for a drink tonight, I made sure to tell her not to dress up. I was going to take her to my local pub and see just how well she coped with my stomping grounds.

After all, I can't keep paying a fortune to take her to fancy restaurants. Her daddy's money will run out soon enough without me using it to woo Theodore Swain's daughter!

No, if she wants Matthias Langdon, Fenella will just have to take me as I am and that means enjoying a drink in the Rose and Crown!

Walking into the village pub, I put a guiding arm to the small of Fenella's back and walked with her up to the bar. "Hi Shirley, do you know Fenella Swain?" I introduced, and watched the two women size each other up.

"Pleased to meet you, I'm sure," Shirley cocked her mouth into half a smile then turned her attention back to me. "Want the usual?" she asked, her smile wide and her eyes animated.

I could see that Fenella was steaming at my side, waiting for me to get the drinks and move to a nearby table. But I didn't – handing her the glass of white wine she had asked for, Fenella was stunned when I patted a barstool next to me, inviting her to sit on it.

"Matt, perhaps-" But Fenella was cut off by Shirley's derisive laughter.

"What's wrong, sugar, you never sat on a barstool before?" Shirley was smirking at her, a drawn on eyebrow lifted in question.

Not wanting to appear stuck up, Fenella raised her chin and put a foot on the lower bar of the stool then hoisted herself onto the seat. "What a great vantage point..." Fenella smiled at me a little triumphantly then looked around at her surroundings, "...it's nice to be able to enjoy the full flavour of the company."

Shirley turned her nose up and marched off up the bar to serve a waiting customer.

Leaning close, I put my mouth to Fenella's ear, "Good one – Shirley can be a bit bitchy now and then, but I think you dealt with her quite nicely."

Enjoying his closeness, Fenella put a hand to Matt's arm and turned her face to place a kiss on his unsuspecting lips. Then she laughed with glee at his stunned look and heard Shirley slam the till drawer shut.

Good, now you know he's mine!

"So this is what you've been up to..." Wesley Craemer walked into the bar and gave Shirley a nod, "...no wonder I haven't seen you in here for a while."

"Wes, good to see you – this is-"

"Fenella Swain," Wes finished for me, and took her hand bringing it to his lips. "And what is m'lady doing in a place like this – not your usual hang out?"

Giggling nervously, Fenella again lifted her chin and said, "Well, from now on it just might be; got a problem with that?"

Watching from the side-lines, I had to admire Fenella's ability to stand up for herself while not alienating the company.

"Oh no, majesty..." and Wes did a comical bow, "...I'm just a poor and lowly farm boy – which reminds me, what the heck are you doing with him?" And Wes jerked a thumb in my direction.

Straightening from the bar, I moved to put an arm around Fenella's waist and said, "She's got good taste in men is why, so keep your hands, and your eyes, off!"

Enjoying the feel of Matt's arm around her and his declaration that she belonged to him, Fenella found herself truly enjoying the unexpected company of Matt's closest friend.

"I don't think I'm quite Wesley's type," Fenella chuckled softly. "I went to university and have a degree in English Literature – I hear Wesley likes his women to have a little more air than brain between their ears."

I laughed loudly at Wesley's wounded expression.

"What lies have you been telling?" Wes asked, his hangdog eyes the picture of innocence.

"It wasn't Matt," Fenella interceded. "It was just a bit of talk amongst us girls – you have quite the reputation," Fenella told Wes with a mischievous grin.

"And well deserved," I exclaimed firmly, tightening the arm around Fenella's waist for just an instant.

"Well, if all you're going to do is besmirch my good name I'm going to sit down in a corner, all by my lonesome, and drink my beer," Wesley complained, and picked up his pint.

"Don't go..." Fenella reached out a hand to touch Wesley's arm and gave him a warm smile, "...I was hoping you might have a few stories about Matt you could tell me."

"Well, if it's secrets you're after I can dish the dirt with the best of them," Wes grinned wickedly and gave me a wink. "Like the time me and Chad caught you and Pam snogging in a barn," Wes laughed, not noticing Fenella's eyes flick quickly to me and then away.

Coughing as I swallowed beer the wrong way, I eventually made to protest. "We were all of 11 or 12 at the time," I recalled, my cheeks hot with embarrassment.

"She's always been keen on our Matt," Wesley informed Fenella, then finally noticed her discomfort. "But it was only a crush — just puppy love really," he assured her, backtracking quickly.

Picking up her wine, Fenella drained the glass then wordlessly handed it to me for a refill.

Our eyes locked for just an instant, Fenella managing to convey her displeasure quite clearly in that brief look.

While Shirley took care of my order, Fenella turned her attention back to Wesley. "That was quite a revelation – do you think Pam still has designs on Matthias?"

Looking a little sheepish, Wesley decided that honesty, with a dash of tact, was the best policy. "I don't think she's ever given herself a chance to like anyone else – Pam has always had tunnel vision where Matt's concerned."

"Have you ever taken Pam out?" Fenella asked, taking the fresh glass of wine that I held out to her, noticing that I too looked interested in Wesley's answer.

"Wouldn't look twice at me," Wes shrugged and took a swig of his beer.

"So you tried then?" I persisted with a frown.

"Not really – oh alright...yes, but not seriously..." Wes confessed reluctantly, "...just asked her out for a drink."

"Jesus man, is no woman safe from you?" I shook my head in disgust.

"Not jealous are you darling?" Fenella asked with a raised brow.

"Of course not – just can't get over the cheek of it," I told her, putting my arm back around her waist and giving Fenella a gentle squeeze. "She deserves a lot better than him," I declared, raising my beer glass in Wesley's direction.

"Gee thanks, with mates like you who needs enemies," Wes frowned, then grinned over at me and raised his glass. "To best buds," he toasted, and we chinked glasses both grinning like fools.

Tutting loudly, but only for show, Fenella rolled her eyes and said, "Men – honestly!"

Having dropped Fenella off at home I drove back to the farm and had time to think about our 'date'.

I really don't get what's going on. Swain said I wasn't to tell Fenella about our deal – but why would he force me to date his daughter if Fenella hadn't asked him to arrange it in the first place?

And then there's the whole marriage thing – he's given me six months of dating then we have to get engaged, then married if that's what Fenella wants.

Gees, I must have been crazy to agree to this, but I just couldn't see another way around it. Without his money Swain knows the farm would be lost and I can't let that happen...even if it does mean an arranged marriage.

Pulling up in front of the farmhouse, I did a quick walk around the property checking the stables and the general area. It all seemed to be in order so I went indoors to get myself a beer. I'd had one pint of beer at the pub and then I'd sat on rock shandies for the last couple. It was no better than drinking pop but at least it gave the illusion of drinking a beer.

Not bothering to pour the drink into a glass, I took the can into the sitting room and flopped into an armchair.

I was feeling guilty – I had always seen myself with Pam, even though neither one of us had actually spoken of it out loud. It just seemed to be the accepted thing – or maybe I was reading the situation all wrong.

My world had turned upside down in such a short

space of time. One minute I was living the dream, running the farm and making a decent job of it...the next...well...

If I hadn't allowed my customers to build up so much credit I wouldn't be in this mess – and then, of course, I had to pay out for all that feed and supplies. With nothing coming in I didn't have it to pay out.

But I would have, if Macey and the rest had just given me some time, damn it! He's never been such a stickler in the past – but then maybe he has the right idea – I don't imagine Macey will ever find himself in my position.

In truth, I had learned a lot this past few months since Chad had gone and I'd had to learn to balance the books. I hadn't liked chasing up late payments, knowing how hard the economy was affecting everyone in the business, but I'd be keeping on top of it from now on.

Damned supermarkets take their own sweet time to pay their bills – what if I was to take my own sweet time in supplying them with my best beef; then we'd see who's chasing who!

Finishing off the can of beer, I walked out to the kitchen to put it in the bin. For a while I just stood looking out the window across the land that my family have owned and farmed for so many years. My great, great, great grandfather had started it all – Arthur Langdon had been a man of the land and had managed to eke out a good living.

It was his son, Chadwick Langdon, after whom Chad had been named, who set about buying up the surrounding land. As now, farming had gone through tough times and when a farmer wanted to sell up and move on, Chadwick Langdon had been able to purchase the land cheap.

Langdon farm reached right down to the outskirts of the village, though the far acreage was set to grazing for the beef stock.

In terms of acreage, Langdon farm was three times larger than even the Swain residence – but then, Swain didn't farm his land. A few years ago he'd built a few large houses on the land nearest the village and made a huge profit, the rest was set aside for Fenella's horses and her mother's lovely garden.

However, Swain money came from their main business, a well established and popular newspaper.

I remember when the Swain's bought their farm – it didn't take them long to cash in on the land. Those houses he built were well out of the local's price range – nothing more than executive housing!

Typical rich man's way of thinking – if I'd been doing a building project it would've been to provide affordable homes for the youngsters in these parts. So many have to move away if they want to get onto the property ladder –

even renting isn't much of an option, just not enough houses to go around.

That night the germ of an idea began to take hold in my thoughts. By the time I got up the next morning it had fully taken hold.

Searching out Mac, I found him in the hay barn getting ready to load up the trailer on the new tractor.

"Don't attach that..." I shouted over to the farmhand now standing watching my approach, "...we're going to use the tractor to take us down to the south field – I want your opinion on something."

"Right you are," Mac nodded amenably, pushing his old cap back on his head. "Do we need to take anything with us?" he asked by way of finding out the purpose of our outing.

"No, not a thing." I strode around the tractor and jumped up into the driver's seat. "Might as well get to drive this damned thing - it's caused us enough trouble."

Nodding again, Mac cracked his weathered face into a smile. "Well, when you ordered it we were expecting to get paid on time for the last lot of beef stock we delivered – can't predict how we'll get paid these days."

"Damned straight," I agreed. "Still, I have an idea that might give us more of a backup pot so that we don't find ourselves in that kind of dire straits ever again!"

"How's it working out for you with Jackson – is he pulling his weight and doing what you tell him?" I asked, though I hadn't seen any signs of disharmony.

"Oh yes, boss – no problem there. My lad was brought up on a farm – my father's land – we lost it in the last recession," Mac recalled though he didn't often dwell on the past – a waste of time in his mind.

"Yes, I remember my father telling me about that." I looked sideways at Mac but saw no sign of upset. "That must have come as quite a blow, though I know my father was glad you came along when you did – expanding into beef cattle in addition to keeping the dairy herd was proving hard work even with two growing lads to help him out."

"Two lads and the little miss," Mac reminded me. "Ashton has always pulled her weight even if her heart lay in riding horses – she never shirked her chores."

I could hear the fond note in Mac's voice – he'd never had a daughter of his own and I thought maybe Ashton was a favourite for that reason.

"Credit where it's due..." I nodded in agreement, "...my sister always got her jobs done before taking off."

"She seems to have settled into that academy alright," Mac observed as we pulled up for him to undo the last gate leading to the south field. "Said she's been working the clock round — what with the stable work, the riding lessons and the competitions — but I can tell Ashton's enjoying it all despite the odd grumble in her letters."

I blinked in surprise, "She's been writing to you?"

Shifting uncomfortably in his seat, Mac felt his cheeks heat up, "Just the odd note now and then — said she would when she left."

We jumped down from the tractor and looked around at the large herd of grazing cattle.

"That's good — though she doesn't get around to writing to me very often," I frowned. "Too busy enjoying herself. Still, I wouldn't want it any different — Ashton deserves a chance to make it big in the sport she loves."

CHAPTER EIGHT

Together, Mac and I stood looking around the large field at the grazing cattle until I finally got to the point of our visit.

"I've been thinking about the village, the youngsters who end up moving away because they can't afford property prices when the odd cottage does come up for sale," I began, looking beyond the stone walls to the village that was within easy walking distance from the bottom of the field.

"Aye, well, it was hoped that the Swain constructions would allow for at least a few affordable properties..." Mac frowned unhappily, "...but, as you know, they were all so high priced no one in the village could afford them. Swain sold them all to his rich pals, not even lived in all year round – like most of the cottages those city people buy – only used as holiday homes.”

“Exactly! But I have a plan to remedy that,” I told him, pursing my lips with determination. “Do you remember Sykes, the builder who worked for Swain?”

Grimacing Mac nodded looking sideways at me with his brows drawn together in question.

“Well, he approached me at the same time as he was working for Swain – said he could make us both a mint of money if I was willing to sell him this bottom field.”

“And you’re thinking about doing that?” Mac looked askance, hardly able to believe his ears.

“No, I’m not,” I replied hastily, and watched Mac’s shoulders relax in relief. “But I am planning to build some affordable housing for local people on this field.”

“But this field alone is 5 acres – that’s a lot of grazing land you’d be losing,” Mac cautioned, but I could see he liked the idea of what I was trying to achieve. “And what about your father – do you reckon he’d approve?”

“I don’t know, but the farm is mine now, free and clear,” I stated proudly. “Both Ashton and Chad signed it over to me – neither one of them wants any part of it.”

“I was shocked when Chad did that,” Mac admitted.

“Yes, so was I,” I agreed, looking off into the distance as if I might see Chad if I looked hard enough. “I always imagined us running the farm together – he was always such a natural at it. I've had to run to catch up since he left, but I think I'm starting to get the hang of things."

"You're doing just fine," Mac encouraged, then turned away with embarrassment.

"Thanks, that means a lot," I smiled, bemused by the pride I felt at getting the older man's approval.

"So...have you talked to anyone yet – architects and such," Mac asked, and raised his hand to stroke one of the cows that had walked over to him.

"Not yet, I've only recently given it serious thought and I wanted to run it by you – see if you thought it was a practical idea," I explained.

"Well, I don't know anything about building houses, but I do know the village has a need of them," Mac rubbed his chin thoughtfully. "And the farm has plenty enough land to move the herd – more than enough really. I know your dad considered selling some of it off when times got hard – but he said he felt he'd be selling his children short if he didn't pass on the full family legacy."

"He did? Well that makes me feel a lot better about the idea." I blew out a heavy breathe in relief. "It won't come as so much of a shock if dad's already considered it."

"I reckon the planning department will go for it too," Mac added, now considering the idea more seriously.

"Especially if the houses are earmarked for locals — imagine the growth it would promote — business and community would benefit from it."

Riding her palomino horse, Fenella was enjoying the good weather and thinking over her night out with Matt.

I don't know why I'm so wound up — it isn't like Matt was the one who brought Pam's name up — but his reaction to Wesley having asked her out wasn't what I expected.

He was out with me, for heaven's sake — that should be enough to satisfy me. But it isn't. Matt seemed to smile at all the right times, kept the conversation going and even had his arm around me, but all the time I had this feeling that he didn't want to be there.

Turning her horse to face a row of jumps, Fenella cantered towards them and took them easily.

Maybe I'm just getting paranoid — since I found out he took Camille out I seem to imagine him with every damned female in the district — especially Pam!

Going around again, Fenella lined up the jumps and again took them with ease. Gilded Lady was a very experienced jumper; Fenella had won many competitions riding her favourite horse.

"Good girl," she smiled, patting the horse's neck affectionately.

Not ready to return Gilded Lady to her stable, Fenella headed out across a field that abuts Wesley Craemer's father's land.

Riding to the bordering fence, Fenella spotted Wes riding Titan and admired his easy grace. She'd never fancied Wes; having watched him from a distance since her father had bought the neighbouring farm to his, Fenella had formed the opinion that he was a shallow womaniser.

"Though what they ever see in you is beyond me," she thought aloud. "You might have a pretty face but you have no respect for women!"

She knew that Matt's farm also abutted Wes', but from the opposite side. Fenella often thought that was a shame, if Matt had lived next door she might have gotten to know him sooner and have had better access to him.

Little 'Pammie' has all the access she needs – the blasted woman works for Matt!

Getting seriously rattled by that thought, Fenella dug her heels into the horse's side and took off at breakneck speed back across the field.

"Hey, what's the matter, Princess?" her father wanted to know as she came to a halt on the opposite side of the fence that surrounded the car park.

"Nothing," she sulked unconvincingly. "You going into work?"

Standing by his Mercedes with the door open, Theo considered just agreeing that he was and waving his daughter goodbye – but if there was one thing he couldn't stand, it was to see his 'princess' upset.

Closing the car door, he walked over to the fence and stroked the palomino's head as she lowered it to him.

"I was, but I don't have to if there's something you need to discuss with me," he offered.

"It's nothing," Fenella told him as she dismounted and tied the mare's reins to the fence. "I'm just out of sorts."

"Hmm..." Theo put an arm around his daughter as she joined him and they walked towards the house, "...would this have anything to do with Matthias Langdon – I thought the two of you were dating?"

"Yes, we are...well, sort of," Fenella sighed.

Stopping and turning his daughter to face him, Theo frowned down with concern. "You're either dating or you're not – which is it?"

Knowing that her father worried about her, Fenella wasn't surprised by his sudden interest in her love life.

"Oh, it's nothing, daddy," she began, not sure exactly what she could tell him. "It's just...well...I sometimes get the feeling that Matt doesn't really want to be with me. According to Camille, he and Pam have been close since they were little – apparently most people expected them to marry in time."

"Would that be Pamela Hooper?" Theo asked, his brows drawn together in thought.

"Yes, do you know her?" Fenella asked surprised.

"No, no, just heard mention of her is all," her father explained. "Like you said, a lot of the locals see them as an item; I just caught the gist of a conversation when I was in the village a while ago."

"Oh, so you already know what I'm talking about," Fenella sighed heavily. "I don't think I really stand a chance while she's around – did you know that 'Pammie' actually works for Matt in his stables?"

"No, I didn't," and Theo considered what he could do about that situation. "But maybe she'll move on to pastures new and leave you with a clear field."

Laughing at her father's choice of words, Fenella gave his arm a hug. "You're really getting into this country living thing," she chuckled as her father realised what he'd just said. "Pastures new and clear field – you'll be writing a country file column in your own paper before long."

"Now then, no making fun of your father, it isn't nice," Theo warned playfully.

"Ok," Fenella smiled, cheered up by her father's loving attention. "Now get off to work, I'll be fine...really."

When Theo got behind the wheel of his Mercedes he wasn't thinking about his newspaper business. *I think I need to make Ms Hooper an offer she can't refuse, and if she does...well...there are other ways of getting rid of her!*

Having arranged a meeting with Sykes, the builder, I headed down to the south field to meet him. Mac and Jackson had already shifted the beef herd into another grazing field, so we had a clear view of the whole field.

Unsurprisingly Sykes was already there when I arrived and had his notebook and pen out, scribbling furiously.

"You beat me to it – not late am I?" I looked at my watch knowing that I was in fact early. "No, no, it appears I'm early – just how early were you?"

I wasn't angry, just a bit annoyed by the builder's eagerness. On the telephone, Sykes had gone into overdrive once I'd expressed my interest in building on the land that the builder had once offered to buy.

Beaming with enthusiasm, Sykes held his hand out to me as I walked over to greet him. "Can't let the grass grow under our feet on this one, hey," Sykes laughed heartily at his own joke. "I've just been working out how many houses we could get on this site – best to maximise quantity to maximise profit. Now then, will you be offering a few executive homes along with the lower end of the market?"

Shaking my head, I stuck to my guns on the plan for affordable housing only. "I already told you, this land is for local occupation — all of the homes will be two or three bedrooms and have a decent sized garden for family use. I'm not in the business of catering to the rich — and this is a one-time deal, got it!"

In his enthusiasm, Sykes had spent much of the time on the phone with Matt trying to persuade the landowner to part with even more land. But Matt had stuck firm.

"I know what you said, but I could show you figures that would make the proposition truly irresistible," Sykes grinned, almost maniacally. "You could provide the local population with the housing it needs and throw in a handful of executive properties that I could sell for around £450-£600K each! Think of the new farming equipment you could buy — the latest tractor...and whatever else a farmer could wish for!"

"I just got a new tractor," I informed him, and looked Sykes directly in the eyes, mine hard and unyielding. "If you can't get on board with this plan I'll find another builder who can — I will not be building on any more of my land and I will certainly not be building any flashy executive homes — got it now!"

Realising that I was deadly serious and that he was in danger of losing the lucrative contract, Sykes backtracked quickly.

"As a contractor I am obliged to point out the best use

of land to ensure that my client receives the best return on their investment," Sykes assures me, as though he had only ever had my best interests at heart. "But if that is what you want, I will most certainly get my architect to draw up the plans accordingly — no need to look for another builder," he added hopefully.

"Good, then we're on the same page at last," I frowned, looking around the field and imagining the houses and families that would soon occupy it.

It'll be nice to do something for the village — to give something back for all the years of good living this land has given my family. I don't think Arthur Langdon would disapprove — he loved this land and the community that surrounded it. Though Chadwick Langdon the first might not be so thrilled — he was the one who acquired most of our land, buying up surrounding farms as they were going under.

"Yes, it's time to give something back," I stated aloud, causing Sykes to look at me curiously. "When you've had time to brief your architect I want a meeting with him to discuss design and size of the houses. I don't want to build rabbit hutches that are depressing spaces to live in!"

"Well no..." Sykes half ran to keep up with my long legged stride, "...but we don't want to be too generous — think how many more local people you will be able to house," he added obsequiously.

"Set a meeting up with your architect as soon as possible..." I instructed before hoisting myself up into the seat of my new tractor, "...I'll want to approve any plans before they're submitted to the planning office."

On the drive back up to the main house, I thought about the housing venture I'd just begun.

I had no idea how much the land was worth with planning permission. Hell, I've only got provisional planning consent and it was estimated at £3M. It seems we owe a huge debt of thanks to great granddaddy Chadwick – if it weren't for his fiscal abilities way back then, we wouldn't be looking at keeping our farm while making enough money to keep us comfortable for the rest of our lives.

Won't Chad and Ashton be surprised! And I chuckled to myself as I made plans for sharing the profit from this venture with my siblings.

Signing over the farm to me was one thing – I can't profit from selling off the land as housing without sharing those profits with them. We'll all be set for life if we use the money wisely. I just wish Chad would get in touch – I think he'd enjoy being in on this project; fact is he has a better business brain than I do.

But Chad hadn't been in touch since he'd left the farm

after breaking up with Fallon Craemer, the daughter of the farmer whose land abutted their own.

He'd never discussed the breakup with me and I had never asked Fallon what had happened – it just seemed too rude and insensitive to do so. But I'd wondered about it – had hoped that once Chad had calmed down a bit he'd be back. But months had passed with no word from my brother and I knew how stubborn Chad could be.

If Chad wanted to disappear off the face of the earth, there would be no finding him, so I hadn't tried.

Be safe, brother, and come home soon.

CHAPTER NINE

Two days later, I got my dearest wish. Coming down for an early breakfast before starting the day's work, I found Chad already sat at the kitchen table with a bowl of cornflakes half eaten in front of him.

"What the hell?!" I stood stock still, then moved across the room and into my brother's open arms. "Chad – I can't believe you're home – it's so good to see you!"

"Not my home anymore..." Chad reminded me, patting my back then breaking away to retake his seat, "...it's yours now, free and clear."

"This will always be home for you and Ashton – it doesn't matter what it says on the deeds," I assured him.

"Good to know, but I'm not sure how long I'll be staying," Chad frowned, contemplating his cereals.

"You're not staying?" I was stunned. I'd missed my

brother in the worst way and thought he'd come back —
but now he was talking about leaving again. "Why — you
always loved this farm — why would you choose to leave
it?"

"For the same reasons I left in the first place," Chad's
frown deepened but he didn't fill me in on what those
reasons had been.

"I see. Well, I need to get on — your room will need
airing and the bed will want making up," I told my brother
stiffly. "Just don't leave without saying goodbye this
time!"

Then I was out the door and crossing the yard to the
milking shed where Mac and Jackson had already started
cleaning the cows ready to start the morning milking.

Mac and Jackson gave each other a curious look when
I stalked into the shed with a look of thunder in my eyes.

"You alright, boss?" Mac asked with genuine concern.

"God damn the man!" I stormed, kicking the side of an
empty stall. "He leaves without a damned word, then
arrives back the same way — and he's already talking
about taking off again!

"Does that mean Chad is home?" Mac asked for
clarification.

"Not for long, according to him!" I kicked the stall
again and wished I hadn't when my big toe started to
throb.

"Then there's hope he might stay," Mac tried to be upbeat. "Once he's settled in maybe Chad will get a feel for the land again - like he did when you were boys."

Not given to fits of temper, I smiled at the memory. "Yeah, you're right, maybe he will." But I couldn't help thinking, *As long as Fallon doesn't come back into the equation, that is. I don't know what happened between them but I don't want her messing with his head again right now. Mac's right – once Chad gets his hands in the soil again he'll remember what's really important to him. I hope!*

By the time the milking was done and I walked round to the stables, Pam was there working and Ronan was gone from his stall.

"Where's Ronan?" I asked Pam, but thought I already knew the answer.

"Hey, you didn't tell me Chad was back," Pam grinned over as I walked towards her. "He took Ronan out a few minutes ago – that blessed horse was all excited to see him," she grinned and rolled her eyes to the heavens.

"Why does that not surprise me?" I shook my head and looked out on the track my brother would have taken. "Those two are kindred spirits – both stubborn, prideful and mean as hell if you get on the wrong side of them – they understand each other," I added quietly.

Moving to put a hand on my arm, Pam stood looking up at me and waited for me to look back at her. "Is something wrong – did you and Chad have a fight?"

"Not exactly," I sighed, automatically placing a hand over the one on my arm and grazing my thumb over it. "I was so happy to see him but right off the bat he told me he probably won't be staying long."

My heavy sigh told Pam more than my words had; I was hurting and she wanted to comfort me.

Without thinking about it, Pam moved round front of me, reached up behind my head and pulled me down for a kiss that would blow both of us away.

It was like dynamite going off in our heads – for years we had wanted this but neither of us had been brave enough to step over the friendship line for fear of the repercussions.

But Pam was past that now – if Fenella Swain wanted her man she wasn't just going to stand by and let her take him. From now on Pam would be fighting back!

But then the unthinkable happened – Matt put her firmly away from him then stood staring at Pam like he was disgusted by what they'd just done.

Pam's thoughts are desperate. Don't look at me like that – don't you feel it – don't you feel like you are home at last? I love you, Matthias Langdon, and I know you felt something for me just then. You don't kiss someone you don't care for like that – you are as hungry for me as I am for you, damn it!

But Matt destroyed her even more when he said, "That must never happen again...ever," then turned and strode out of the stable yard away from her.

When Chad got back from his ride, he set Ronan loose in the paddock and carried his saddle into the tack room.

"What the hell?" he asked, finding Pam sobbing her heart out quietly in a corner of the room. Taking a seat beside her, Chad put an arm across her shoulders and pulled her in for a hug. "Come on now, tell uncle Chad all about it," he quipped trying to make her smile.

But Pam was in bits, broken by a look that shattered her heart and her dreams. "I love him, Chad, I always have," Pam sniffed into her tissue. "I always thought he felt the same way – he always acted as though he did – we just couldn't seem to cross the friendship line...but...but..."

A whole new torrent of tears and sobs began racking Pam's body as Chad held her close.

"I gather we're talking about Matt here?" he asked, shaking his head at his brother's idiocy. The lad had been mooning after Pam since they were kids and Chad had seen the way he'd looked at her when she'd become full grown.

My pea-brained brother needs a good talking too, Chad told himself as Pam nodded her confirmation.

But Chad would have to wait in line – not only was Matt beating himself up over his inappropriate behaviour, Mac had witnessed the scene and was looking daggers at him.

"I didn't start it," I defended myself when Mac continued to work silently beside me, the air between us heavy with disapproval.

"Not my place to have opinions one way or the other," Mac stated brusquely, but managed to make me squirm just the same.

"Damn it! I've kept my hands off Pam for years – I know anything between us will just bring trouble – but when she kissed me..." I tailed off; remembering that kiss was seriously distracting. "It was everything I knew it would be."

Putting down the bale of hay he'd just picked up to stack along with the rest, Mac turned to look at me with a quizzical frown creasing his weathered brow.

"You two have been sweet on each other since you were kids – how the hell did you get mixed up with the likes of Fenella Swain?" Mac asked, crossing a line that minutes earlier he'd sworn to himself he wouldn't.

"It's complicated," I told him. "Let's just say, I didn't

go looking for her – it just...sort of happened."

But now that Mac had crossed the line between employee and concerned friend, he wasn't going to back away from the issue as he saw it.

"I know the bank turned you down for a loan..." Mac admitted, watching me pale at his revelation, "...I've lived here most of my life – people talk." When I made no move to deny his statement, Mac decided to push on. "Theodore Swain can be very persuasive – what Fenella wants Theo usually finds a way to buy it. Is that what happened, Matt?"

Shrugging, I was tempted to deny it, but what was the point when Mac already seemed to have it all worked out. "I was desperate – and it's just a loan," I assured the man who had been like a second father to me.

Nodding, Mac picked up the bale at his feet and slung it up onto the top of the pile he and I had been building. "A loan with strings I'm guessing."

Then I blurted out the whole deal – courtship, engagement and marriage – the whole nine yards!

"That bloody man has more money than sense!" Mac declared angrily. "And you don't have the sense you were born with," he growled, pushing a hand through his bushy greying hair. "Don't you know who you're getting involved with – Theodore Swain is one of the dirtiest businessmen

I've had the displeasure to come across?"

Taken aback, I shook my head. "I've never heard anything bad about him."

"You wouldn't have!" Mac let out a long exasperated breath. "Your father was a canny man, he knew better than to get involved with someone like Swain. But I've heard from others in the village – suddenly the bank can't help them when their cash-flow is flowing the wrong way for a time – then in steps Swain with his offer of help, only it comes with a mess of strings attached."

"Strings?" I asked.

"Yes, bloody strings," Mac confirmed angrily. "Swain uses that newspaper of his to gather info on people. According to some, he isn't above using it to blackmail someone into doing as he wants – whatever he wants," Mac added ominously.

"Well...hopefully Sykes will get the planning permission we need to crack on with the housing project then I can pay Theodore Swain back with interest!"

Studying the young man before him Mac worried that disentangling himself from Swain may not be as straight forward as Matt seemed to believe.

Before either of us could comment further I saw Chad striding towards the barn. "Say nothing," I demanded in low tones to Mac, then turned to watch my brother close the gap between us.

"I leave you on your own for five bloody minutes and you get yourself so tangled up with women that you don't know your arse from your thick head," Chad ranted angrily.

"You've been gone a lot longer than five minutes," I scoffed somewhat belligerently. "As for the women in my life, it's my life, stay out of it!"

Mac stood to one side watching us square up to each other. He'd had to break us up when we were boys scrapping in the field, but he didn't fancy coming between us now we were grown men.

"You arsehole! Pam is breaking her heart over you and all you can do is act the big man," Chad sneered bitterly. "If you weren't interested in Pam you shouldn't have led her on – love isn't something that can be switched on and off like a bloody tap!"

"Really – you're one to talk," I snapped back, too angry now to watch my words.

"What the fuck does that mean?!" Chad's eyes had gone black with rage and his voice was so low it was little more than a guttural growl.

"Fallon – she's the reason you took off," I stated and watched the low blow hit home when Chad paled. "You're no better with women than I am so don't try to make out like your some kind of expert – you ran away, I'm still here."

There was no warning – the two of us went at each other like raging bulls. Fists pounded and thudded into flesh, then we were rolling on the ground trying to knock seven bells out of each other.

"What the hell...!" It was Jackson, he'd just come in from the fields to find us fighting. "Shouldn't we break this up?" he asked Mac.

"Give them a minute to get the worst of it out of their systems then we'll take one each," Mac frowned and sighed heavily.

While we were rolling around on the ground the blows that landed were mainly ineffectual, but as we worked our way back to our feet the power of our blows increased.

I landed a fist that caused Chad's nose to pour with blood and he let out a growl that any grizzly bear would be proud of. As Chad lunged at me Mac gave Jackson the nod and they waded in to pull us apart.

Jackson pinned Chad's arms to his side - his arms encircling Chad's heaving chest like steel bands. "Take it easy – just calm down," Jackson advised, watching his dad drag me away and restrain me.

"Get the hell off me!" Chad roared angrily, struggling to free himself and get back to pounding on me.

"Not until you two calm down," Mac replied, still

holding onto me, and I was still raging. "You're grown men – whatever your differences get them settled as such, not like a pair of schoolboys!"

Both of us seemed to sag a bit at Mac's remonstration, recalling the brawls he'd broken up years before.

Looking at Mac, Chad gave a nod and Mac gave his son a signal to let him go. "What about you..." he asked me, "...are you done?!"

I nodded my head and Mac freed me from the arm-lock he had me in, but father and son still watched us warily.

With his face and shirt covered in blood Chad strode wordlessly away, going back to the house and leaving me to face Mac's wrath.

"Damn it!" I shook my hand, glaring at my painful knuckles.

Although I was his boss, Mac had been working for my father before me and had known me since I was in nappies. That gave him some leeway in the boss employee relationship.

Grabbing my hand and causing me to grimace with pain, Mac examines the knuckles and fingers declaring them unbroken. "Jesus, I thought you two had gotten past the fighting stage – don't you think he'd better understand if you explained things to him?

"No!" I snapped stubbornly. "And I don't want you saying anything to him either!"

Holding up a hand, Mac shook his head. "You told me in confidence, I don't break confidences."

Looking Mac in the eyes, I nodded, "Good enough. I suppose we'd better sort this lot out."

There were hay bales and feed scattered around us. *Trust us to knock over the only open sack!*

CHAPTER TEN

It was becoming more and more difficult to motivate myself to call Fenella. After the kiss with Pam, I just didn't have the heart to cheat on her. And no matter how I told myself that I was being stupid, in my heart of hearts, I knew I wasn't.

This situation is getting worse by the day. I can hardly bare to look at Pam the way she's hurting – and I did that! But I don't know how to get out of this fix. There's no good in telling Pam that I love her only to go off and marry Fenella!

I don't even have the money to pay Swain back yet – at least if I did I could talk to him about dropping the deal – surely he wouldn't force me to marry his daughter, what would Fenella think about that if she found out?

But then, maybe she already knows. I know Theo told

me I wasn't allowed to tell Fenella about the deal, but that doesn't mean she hadn't asked her 'daddy' to fix things for her. He always did – no matter what Fenella wanted he found a way to get it for her. Is that what happened – did she tell her father that she wanted me and he found a way to force my hand.

He'd know how to do it too. There's no way I'd let the farm slip through my fingers – had he had something to do with that call the bank received while I was there asking for a loan? It was weird how one minute we were going to talk about how the bank could help me, then after that call they couldn't get rid of me fast enough.

Something is really off about all of this!

Taking Symphony out of her stall, I saddled her up and walked her into the stable yard.

"Will you be long?" Pam asked, not raising her eyes enough to meet mine. "Only we have lessons starting in an hour and I usually use Symphony for my advanced riders."

"I'll be back before then," I told her, then swung myself up into the saddle and walked the mare as far as the field. After that I let her have her head, the wind warm against my face as I allowed myself to forget.

Even though I wasn't as avid a rider as Chad and Ashton, I still enjoyed the solitude and peace that I found when I did take one of the horses out.

Without thinking about where I was going, I found myself one fence away from the Craemer farmhouse.

Taking it easily, I patted Symphony's neck in congratulations as we trotted towards the main doors.

"Ok girl…" I crooned, tying the mare's reins to a fencepost, "…I won't be gone long." But I made sure she had enough length in the reins to be able to graze if she wanted to.

With a farewell pat I strode up to the front door and rang the ancient bell. When Fallon opened the door she looked surprised to see me.

"Not disturbing you in the middle of something am I?" I asked, uncharacteristically nervous.

"Don't be silly," Fallon chastised with a smile and a wave of her hand for me to go in. "You haven't been over in a while – why is that?"

"Work," I stated feeling easier now that I was inside the familiar kitchen. I'd eaten meals in this kitchen almost as many times as I had in my own home. "How are you, Mrs Craemer?" I asked the older woman by the stove.

"I'm fine, Matt – have you heard from your mum and dad lately? I can still hardly believe they went off gallivanting at their age – still, what I wouldn't give for a holiday," she grinned, and picked up another tray of muffins putting them into the oven alongside the ones I'd watched her put in when I'd arrived.

But I knew Mrs Craemer was happiest when she was looking after someone. If she wasn't cooking for her own family she was cooking for some charity or a neighbour that wasn't in good health.

At least she doesn't have to cook for us anymore – me Chad and Ashton just about ate her out of house and home when we were kids...but we were always made welcome.

"I heard from them a couple of days ago," I informed her with a smile. "They're in Egypt now – something about mum having always wanted to see the pyramids. Dad doesn't sound too impressed though, said behind the touristy places there's a lot of poverty."

"I think you'll find pockets of that everywhere," Mrs Craemer sighed. "We have areas of poverty in this country too – much more than the government likes to admit to."

Just then, Wes walked into the kitchen and found me being served a mug of tea. "Hey, where's mine?" he asked in playful umbrage.

"Sit down and I'll pour you a mug," his sister, Fallon, told him. "Though I can make you some strong black coffee if you'd prefer – or a glass of Alka-Seltzer?" she added with a raised eyebrow.

"Just the tea," Wes frowned then turned to look at me. "So, how's things?"

"You look like death warmed up," I told him instead of answering the polite inquiry. "Out late?"

"No..." Fallon answered ahead of her brother, "...he just got home early – around 5 a.m. wasn't it?"

Rolling his eyes at her, Wes picked up the tea she'd just set in front of him and managed to burn his mouth with the first sip. "Bloody hell!"

"You are so trashed!" I laughed at my lifelong friend.

"Yeah, but I had a good time getting this way," Wes grinned happily.

"You intend doing any work today?" his sister asked.

"I pull my weight," Wes nonchalantly waved Fallon's dig aside. "Just give me a minute to get this tea inside me and I'll be ready to start."

I looked at him dubious, but I'd known Wes long enough to know that he wasn't a shirker.

"Where'd you get the shiner?" Wes frowned, pointing at the outer edge of my right eye.

"Chad – but I gave him a bloody nose," I declared proudly.

A plate fell to the kitchen floor and smashed at Fallon's feet. "Chad's back?"

Shifting uncomfortably in my seat, I looked at Fallon's

shocked face and realised that my brother hadn't been in touch. "Sorry, I thought you knew," I apologised.

Wes looked angry and immediately got to his feet. "I'll get it – just go and sit down a minute."

Fallon did as she was told while Wes got out the dustpan and brush and cleared up the broken plate.

"How long?" Fallon asked.

"Not long," I evaded, not wanting to tell her that it had been over a week. "He looks like shit and goes around like a bear with a sore head – hence the fist-fight," I smiled hopefully, pointing at my eye in a bid to distract her.

"So, the coward can't even be bothered to come and see me," Fallon declared, the colour coming back into her cheeks now that her temper was rising. "Well, if he can't be bothered then neither can I – as far as I'm concerned Chadwick Langdon doesn't exist!"

At first it seemed Fallon was managing to deal with the emotional blow, but when she fled from the kitchen seconds later I was sure I'd seen tears beginning to fall.

"Sorry," I apologised, looking at Mrs Craemer and then at Wes. "My brother can be an insensitive clod at times. Though if it's any consolation, I wasn't kidding when I said he looks like shit – I think he's suffering as badly as Fallon, he's just too pig-headed to admit it."

"Well, if it's meant to be it will be," Mrs Craemer told no one in particular while looking at the empty kitchen doorway after Fallon.

"I'll give him a bloody nose if he doesn't get his arse into gear," Wes snapped angrily. "He could've at least called me so that I could prepare Fallon for the fact that he's back!"

Putting his empty mug in the sink, Wes gave his mum a quick peck on the cheek and a rueful smile. "Your wayward son is going to get some work done – I'll dig out that plot of land you've been asking me to dig for the last who knows how long." Then he looked at me with fire in his eyes, "I could do with some good hard labour to burn off some of this mad!"

Standing, I followed Wes outside and realised that he really was mad when I had to almost run to keep up.

"Hey, it isn't me you're mad at remember," I called after Wes as he rounded the corner of the house to his mother's back garden.

"Maybe not, but you're here!"

Well that says it all, I told myself with a resigned sigh. "I suppose this isn't the time to bend your ear about another problem?" I asked, hoping to distract my friend out of his foul mood.

I hadn't planned to spill the beans on my travesty of a

deal with Theodore Swain, but now I'd thought about it, it didn't seem like such a bad idea.

Wes stopped so suddenly that I almost ran into him. "Is that why you came over – you got a problem?"

"I did – I do," I replied stiltedly. "I've done something really stupid but I can't tell you about it if you're going to blurt it out to Chad in the process of bashing his brains in."

"Huh!" Wes huffed loudly, then took a deep breath and let it out on a long sigh. "You know me better than that, I hope. You tell me something in confidence I don't go blabbing about it to all and sundry. Now spill."

We walked across Mrs Craemer's beautifully kept back garden to sit on a low wall.

"It has to do with why I've been seeing Fenella Swain," I began, and watched my friend raise a brow. "You know how hard it's been for us farmers of late..." I continued, feeling awkward and hesitant to admit that I wasn't as good at managing the farm as Chad had been, "...well, to cut a long story short, I was going to lose the farm if I didn't get my hands on some money fast. I went to the bank – at first I thought they were going to help me, but after getting a call from his head office Carl Morrison wouldn't budge – he said as how we didn't have any previous history of taking out a loan with the bank and therefore we were classed as new customers. According to him, his head office had just put an embargo on handing out loans to any new customers and he wouldn't be able to help me after all."

"That was curious timing," Wes frowned at my story. "So where did you get the money-" Wes broke off suddenly, jumped to his feet and looked down at me in a way that spoke volumes about his level of anger, only now it was aimed directly at me. "You went to Swain!" he exclaimed, his tone nothing short of accusatory. "You went to that gangster in sheep's clothing and asked him for a loan!"

"What...gangster...Theo Swain is not a gangster," I protested, but Mac's previous warning about Swain made me uncertain of this proclamation. "He's always been nice to me and I've never heard anything bad about him," I lied, deciding not to admit that Mac had also agreed with Wes' point of view about our neighbour.

"Well you wouldn't," Wes shook his head on a heavy sigh. "You live in your own tidy little world with the farm at the centre of it. But for us more sociable types – well, let's just say that, in the circles I travel in, Swain's reputation isn't the whiter-than-white one he tries to pull off!"

Dropping my head into my hands, I knew I had to

consider the idea that I was now indebted to some kind of twofaced monster.

"I don't know what to do – I can't tell Chad, he'd kill me before he'd help me!"

Retaking his seat on the wall next to me, Wes considered for a minute. "Look, in the first place, if the bank refused you your next step should have been to come to us," Wes informed me with an annoyed frown. "Our families have always helped each other out – we may not have as many generations on our land but we go back a long way with the Langdon's."

Nodding, shame faced, I silently agreed.

"Ok, so tell me the rest of it," Wes demanded less angrily. "There has to be more to it than just taking out a loan with Swain – what did he get you to do for him in return?"

Actually blushing now, I grimaced as I looked over at my long-time friend. "That's sort of where Fenella comes into it – he made me agree to take her out...and if she wants to get married sometime in the future I have to go through with it."

Jaw dropped and eyes bugging out of his head, Wes looked at Matt like he'd just told him that he'd robbed the money from the bank. Instead he'd basically told him that he'd sold himself to save his family's farm!

"What the fuck?!" Wes didn't swear often, but this was exceptional circumstances. He was back on his feet now, pacing back and forth in front of me. "You are taking Fenella Swain out because her father demanded that you do so – have I got that right?" I nodded, then hung me head in despair. "And, if she decides she wants to keep you until she gets bored, you have to marry her?"

Not lifting my head, I again nodded in agreement.

"God damn it, Matt! You're lucky I'm too trashed to black your other eye or I would, believe me!"

I believed him. Wes had always been like another brother to me, and I'd been stupid not to seek his advice when things were going pear shaped.

"I'm sorry, I just wanted to prove I could handle the farm on my own," I admitted, feeling stupid now I really thought about it.

He could understand that – Wes was two years older than Matt and two years younger than Chad, so he'd always felt in the middle of their rivalry growing up.

"So, this is why you and Pam aren't together?"

"Partly." I felt the colour flood into my cheeks again. "I think I missed the boat on that score – I didn't make a move on her because I didn't want to lose her as a friend if it went wrong. Now I know she wants more I have no right to promise her what I may not be able to deliver."

"As in, you might have to marry Fenella Swain," Wes needlessly spelled it out and watched me nod in agreement. "Jesus, we need to come up with a plan to get you out of this. Even if you had the balls to tell him where to stick his idiotic deal, Swain would never let you just walk away from it," Wes warned me ominously.

"Actually, I may have found a way to do that." I looked up at Wes, a glimmer of hope in my eyes.

"Yeah, how?" Wes asked dubiously.

"You remember Sykes, the builder who built the executive homes on Swain's land?" I asked him, then continued when Wes gave a nod. "Well, I called him about building some affordable housing on the south field — he was ecstatic, to say the least, and agreed to help develop the project with his architect and get the necessary planning."

I went rushing on, sure that I'd found a way to dig myself out of the hole I'd put myself in. "I never knew how much land was worth these days — well, if it's got planning permission, and Sykes told me that we do now," I explained. "So once the houses are built I'll be able to pay Swain back with a good amount of interest and settle my debt to him."

"And you think that will be it — you just hand over the cash and walk away, right? Wrong!" Wes informed me, and watched as my expression fell.

"Then I'll just have to marry her," I declared, my shoulders falling to a new low.

"No. You can't just give your life up because daddy's little girl wants a new toy," Wes stated loudly, his arms flailing about expressively. "Like I said, we need to come up with a plan."

"She's not so bad, you know." I looked at Wes as he sat back down on the wall. "Fenella...she's not as bad as most people seem to think," I explained when Wes looked at me, confusion in his eyes.

"Hah! Bitch of the universe according to some of my friends," Wes declared, somewhat harshly to my mind.

"I know that's the reputation she's got, but I've seen another side to her – Fenella can be quite sweet when you get to know her."

"Good christ, don't tell me you're actually falling for her?!" Wes asked incredulous.

Once again I shook my head. "No, I love Pam but there's no point telling her that if I can't give her the future she deserves. You said it yourself; I can't just walk away from this deal."

"I did, but I didn't say go meekly like a sacrificial bloody lamb!"

Suddenly Wes got up, went to the garden shed and

got out a spade. Then, much to my surprise, he started digging his mother's garden.

"Is that it?" I asked, watching my friend putting his back into the job at hand.

"I think better when I'm working. You get off, I'll let you know what I come up with," Wes told me without so much as looking up.

Walking back to where Symphony was still tied, I took her reins and led the mare to a watering trough. "There you go, have a drink before we get off." Then I looked at my watch and cursed loudly. "Shit! Now I'm for it!"

And so I was — by the time I rode into the stable yard the riding lesson that Pam had told me about was already done.

CHAPTER ELEVEN

The moment Pam's eyes lighted on me she turned and walked in the opposite direction, her temper evident in every step she took.

"Pam, wait," I pleaded, sliding off Symphony's back and quickly tying her reins to a handy post. Then I was off, following Pam into the tack-room. "Pam, I'm sorry — I ended up at Wes' and you know what it's like trying to get away without having at least a cup of tea," I cajoled shamelessly, then decided to try pulling on her heartstrings and told her about Fallon. "I couldn't just walk out after dropping the bombshell that Chad was back — the poor girl was beside herself," I exaggerated wildly, but I could see Pam's rigid spine softening. "I think she could use a friend to talk to," I suggested, and watched Pam give it some thought.

"I had to apologise profusely that Symphony wasn't available!" Pam scowled up at me, but I could see that she wasn't as angry as she had been. "Luckily one of the other students didn't turn up so I managed – but what would I have done if they had – put them on Ronan?!"

"Hell no!" I exclaimed, the thought of a novice riding the demon horse draining the blood from my face. "I really am sorry – it won't happen again...promise."

Unable to stay mad at me for long, Pam sat and patted the seat beside her. "So Fallon is really upset about Chad?" she asked, and looked sad for her friend when I confirmed that she was. "Ok, well, I suppose you couldn't just leave her like that..." she conceded with a small smile, "...I'll drop by and see her after work...maybe take her out for a drink or something."

"That sounds great." I was so relieved to be out of the doghouse with Pam that I grabbed her hand and gave it a squeeze while giving her a beaming smile.

But when Pam responded to my warmth by placing her free hand over mine, I quickly pulled away and got to my feet. "Er...that's good...that's really good," I told her before exiting the tack-room with ungentlemanly speed.

Left dazed and alone, Pam could only watch after Matt unsure of what just happened.

Is it me? Was it something I did? One minute he was

his old self the next he was running away from me like a scolded cat. I have no clue what is going on!

For the rest of that day I stayed well away from the stables – there was plenty enough to do in the office to keep me occupied and away from Pam.

I hadn't set eyes on Chad since our fight, so when he walked into the office, I was surprised and annoyed to see him. "What do you want?"

It wasn't exactly a friendly greeting, but it was the best I could do under the circumstances.

Not bothering to sit down, Chad nailed me with a stare that could freeze hell over. "What the hell have you been doing with the farm's finances?"

"What?! Have you been snooping through the books – you have no right to do that?!" I was furious, the farm was mine now and Chad had no say in what I did anymore.

"I have every right!" Chad declared, his voice on the dangerous side of quiet. "This farm has been in our family going way back to our 3 times great grandfather – so don't expect me to stand by while you let it go to the dogs!"

"I don't expect you to do anything but keep your bloody nose out of my business," I exploded, my temper fuelled by humiliation. But if I expected my brother to give up and go away, I would have to think again.

Eventually, Chad pulled up a chair and made himself comfortable on the opposite side of the desk to me, his arms folded imperiously across his chest.

"I can wait as long as it takes for you to grow some balls and fess up," Chad challenged, his eyes never leaving mine.

"I have nothing to fess up about," Matt denied stubbornly. "What I do or don't do on this farm is none of your business."

But Chad barely even blinked. He didn't move until I finally got to my feet to leave the office.

"You make one move towards that door and I'll flatten you before you can get through it – neither of us is going anywhere until you tell me everything."

And that was it – there was no way around it – if I didn't come clean my brother and I were headed for another fist fight. Or a very long game of statues, and I was in no mood for games.

"It wasn't entirely my fault," I began, and told Chad all about the late payers and their promises to settle up at the end of the month but then actually hadn't. And I told him about the bank, how they'd seemed like they were going to help then backed away like I was a poor risk. Then eventually, finally, I explained about Swain, the loan I'd asked for and even the conditions that Swain had imposed.

"If they'd paid up when they said they were going to, I wouldn't have needed the loan," I reasoned. "And if I'd known how things were going to turn out I obviously wouldn't have bought the new damned tractor – but the old one was well passed being useful!"

Chad knew I was right – our father had bought the old tractor when he'd taken over the farm from his father. That had been a lot of years ago and no matter how we'd patched it up the old tractor had given its last to the Langdon farm.

"So, if I understand you correctly, Swain has roped you into courting his daughter and then, if the conniving little bitch decides she wants to marry you, he gets a new son-in-law – does that about sum it up?" Chad asked sarcastically.

"Mostly."

"Oh, do tell me, what did I get wrong?"

"Fenella isn't a conniving little bitch," I defended staunchly. "You don't really know her-"

"But you do?" Chad butted in impatiently.

"Yes I do. Admittedly I've thought the same way as you in the past, but I don't think Fenella had anything to do with the situation I'm in."

"God...you're so blind I'm surprised it took this long for you to get ensnared by Swain!" Chad got to his feet then walked over to a filing cabinet and took out the farm's accounts.

"What the hell is that supposed to mean?" I demanded, my temper returning.

"It means – if little Ms Swain had nothing to do with it, what made her father think up the idea to tie you to her side in the first place? Or do you think he just decided to get himself the son he never had?" Chad asked sceptically.

"I know what you're saying – Wes said pretty much the same thing," I conceded unwillingly. "But if that's true, why would old man Swain tell me not to breathe a word of our agreement to his daughter – and threaten me with dire consequences if I did?"

Chad suddenly looked concerned – he'd looked out for me all my life so he wouldn't stand by while someone threatened me. "Exactly what did he say?"

"I don't know – something about 'they won't find the pieces if I decide to make you disappear' – some bullshit like that," I smiled somewhat uncertainly now that I'd said the words out loud.

"You really have no idea who Theodore Swain is, do you?"

I shook my head, "It would seem not. Even Mac is aware of his dangerous reputation – I don't know how it got passed me, but it did."

"You say you've spoken to Wes..." and when I nodded, Chad continued, "...so what did he suggest?"

"Actually, he was so trashed this morning I doubt he took it all in. He was digging his mother's back garden when I left," I explained. "Said he thinks better when he's working."

Surprising me, Chad just nodded. "I'll go and have a word – Wes is usually good at thinking things through and coming up with a workable plan."

"Er...I might not do that if I were you," I grimaced at the thought of my brother coming face to face with Fallon. "Maybe you should phone him – arrange to meet Wes down the pub for a pint. In fact, that's what we should do – all three of us should go to the pub for a pint tonight!"

Looking at me with a cocked brow, Chad tried to way up what I wasn't saying. "What's the problem – I can ride Ronan over to Wes' place and talk to him now. Better to get this thing sorted out as soon as possible," he added when I didn't look convinced.

Damn, I was going to have to tell Chad about Fallon's reaction to the news that he was back and Wes' anger on her behalf.

By the time I got through it, I felt like an idiot for not having kept my mouth shut – but how was I supposed to know that my brother was keeping his head down!

On a heavy sigh, Chad got to his feet and hooked his thumbs into his jeans pockets. "I might as well get it over with – Fallon hangs on to her temper like a fur coat on a winter's day – waiting will not lessen the blast of it."

Leaning back in my chair, I watched my brother walk from the room like a condemned man going to the gallows. I almost felt sorry for him – but this was Chad, and as far as I could tell, he deserved at least some of what he had coming.

Later that evening when Chad eventually returned, I took one look at my brother's face and decided that it wasn't a good time to ask questions.

You look whipped! I don't know what the problem is between you and Fallon, but it's eating you alive.

CHAPTER TWELVE

Flopping onto a settee, Fenella swung her legs up to dangle over the end of it and let out a long sigh.

"What's wrong – you want to come into work with me," Theo offered, knowing that his daughter often liked to help out in the office, just not on a permanent basis. "Your mother has a couple of charitable events coming up – you could go with her to the meetings she's got planned for today," he continued when Fenella just shrugged non-committally at his first offer.

Turning on her side to face him, Fenella shook her head, her eyes mirroring her misery for all to see.

"No...that's ok...thank you daddy."

"Come on, Angel, tell daddy what's wrong?"

A tear slipped from her eyes as she looked over at the only man who had ever truly loved her. "I love him, daddy. But I think Matthias is in love with Pam Hooper. He hasn't called in a couple of days – and I know he's busy, what with the crops needing to be brought in..." she excused, trying to be understanding, "...but even when Matt's with me, I don't think his heart is truly in it."

"Is he not treating you right?" Theodore Swain would not have his daughter treated as second rate by anyone. "I thought you were enjoying your dates with Matthias Langdon?"

Wiping at her eyes and giving an unladylike sniff, Fenella gave her father the best smile she could manage. "Matthias treats me like a lady," she assured him. "And that's the problem – there's no passion – no fire in his blood. When Matt kisses me goodnight it's a quick peck and a lovely smile, but nothing more."

"And you think that's because of the Hooper girl?"

"Unfortunately, yes. She has one big advantage over me – she works with Matthias 5 or 6 days a week. I only get to see him when he has the time to remember me," Fenella finished sadly.

"I've got to go," Theo told her, and got to his feet then bent to give his daughter a kiss. "I don't want you mooning around all day making yourself miserable over Matthias Langdon – do you hear me?"

When she gave him a nod and a half-hearted smile,

Theo felt his heart ache for her. "Don't you worry, Matthias will see who the better woman is – he can't be stupid enough to think a little nobody like Pamela Hooper can hold a candle to my girl!"

"Thanks, daddy, I can always count on you to love me." This time her smile was warm and she blew him a kiss goodbye.

While going out to the helipad he'd had built in a field behind the big barn, Theodore Swain gave his daughter's problem some thought. The pilot held his hand up in greeting as Theo climbed into the rear passenger section of the large white helicopter.

I may have to take a more active role in getting my daughter the man she wants. If Matthias Langdon can't see past the end of his nose then maybe I'll have to remove any obstacles in the way. If Fenella wants him then Fenella shall have him – if that means getting rid of Pamela Hooper... Well, I don't think that will be a problem!

Lizzy was enjoying another lesson on Daisy-belle with Pam teaching her the ropes.

"Don't forget those heels," Pam reminded the young girl. "And don't slump your spine – you need good posture if you want to become a good rider."

Giving Pam a nod, Lizzy adjusted her position and actually felt the benefit.

"Yes, that's good, Lizzy – now give her a nudge with your heels to encourage Daisy-belle into a trot."

"You want me to go up and down like I did earlier?" the young stable hand asked.

"I know it's more comfortable to do a rising trot but this time I want you to stay seated and feel the rhythm of your horse's movement," Pam encouraged. "Yes, that's it, relax into the trot and keep your body central."

When Matt walked over to see how the lesson was going, Pam wasn't at all sure what to say to him. He'd been so taciturn of late – at least, that's how it felt to her.

"Hmm, I remember this lesson – I never did like doing a seated trot," I grimaced and watched Lizzy bouncing along. "I suppose you'll have her doing it without stirrups soon?"

"It all helps to teach her proper balance and posture," Pam turned slightly to see Matt's face.

When he smiled at her, Pam's heart gave a huge jolt and she just hoped that one day they would be more comfortable with each other again.

Since she'd kissed him the two had been awkward when on their own – but with Lizzy to talk about the atmosphere wasn't quite so strained.

Not that I was the only one doing the kissing – Matt sure as hell responded with as much enthusiasm as I did!

Glimpsing him out of the corner of her eyes, Pam was finding it difficult to concentrate.

"Have you got lessons booked in today?" I asked, trying not to stare at Pam's neat little bottom in the fitted jodhpurs she wore.

"Yes, and I'll need all six horses!" Turning to face me Pam's face pulled into a warning scowl.

Holding my hands up in surrender, I gave her a boyish grin in return. "I promise not to abscond with Symphony. Surely you've forgiven me by now?"

I watched as Pam's lips twitched and a reluctant smile spread across her lovely face.

"I suppose I have," she replied, then turned back to Lizzy. "And what are you grinning at — keep your mind on what you're doing!"

Lizzy let out a smothered giggle. "You don't scare me anymore," she told Pam bravely. "You're too nice to be really cross."

"Don't you believe it," I chuckled as I got down from the paddock fence. "Ms Hooper can be worse than any school teacher once she's riled." And I was only half joking.

But my warning only caused Lizzy to giggle again and Pam turned to frown at me with pursed lips.

"I'm going to see Mac in the top fields..." I told her

before Pam could get really annoyed at me, "...we're starting the wheat harvest today." With that, I waved a hand and grinned wickedly at Lizzy.

Striding away, I could only wonder how I was going to get my life back on track. Because of the ridiculous agreement I'd made with Theodore Swain, I felt I'd all but signed my life away.

Not that Swain could ever take me to court to enforce the contract – it was more of a gentleman's agreement and one my own code of honour wouldn't allow me to break.

But that doesn't mean I don't want to, despite the fact that Fenella has turned out to be much nicer than her reputation painted her. She just isn't the girl for me.

But even as I thought it, I knew I needed to phone Fenella to arrange another date. If I was going to hold up my side of the bargain it meant taking her out on a fairly regular basis.

For long hours I drove the combine harvester while Mac drove the grain trailer alongside. Our farm had its own medium capacity silo which made harvesting a lot easier. But the hours of work were necessarily long – once the grain was ready to harvest we had to beat any inclement weather or risk losing it.

When, a few days later, I was about to head out to

harvest the last couple of fields of wheat, I was surprised to hear Lizzy calling my name.

I knew the girl liked to arrive early, but then so did Pam and the two worked well together. So why was Lizzy racing up to me instead of going to Pam if she had a problem?

Out of breath and panting, Lizzy put her hands on her knees and just breathed for a moment. "Have you seen Pam? I've looked all around the stable yard – none of the horses are missing so she isn't out riding and I've checked the office in case she was in there too."

Knowing how reliable Pam was, I wasn't too concerned. "She may have car trouble – give her another hour or so and I'm sure Pam will turn up. Just do the jobs you normally would and don't go anywhere near Ronan's stall," I reminded Lizzy yet again.

Rolling her eyes, as young teenagers tend to do when having a rule laid out to them for the umpteenth time, Lizzy nodded and smiled her obedience. "There's some tack needs cleaning and I can get the horses fed and watered," she suggested eagerly. "After that I can start the mucking out."

"I'm sure Pam will be here before you get to that," I reassured the girl. "Jackson will be around if you need anything and Chad is in the house."

Lizzy grimaced, she was easy around everyone but Chad; he frightened her when his dark brows drew together over his equally dark eyes, especially if he was looking at her when they did.

Laughing at her expression, I told her not to worry. "My brother isn't as scary as he looks – his bark is much worse than his bite. Mostly..." I warned but winked to make her smile again.

Going back to the stables, Lizzy set about feeding the horses and giving them fresh water. Then she went to the tack room and got on with her work oblivious to the passing of time. She didn't own a watch or a mobile phone so watching the time wasn't a habit she'd ever gotten in to.

But when Jackson came into the stable yard looking for Pam he was surprised when Lizzy told him that she hadn't seen her yet and the young girl felt guilty and panicked.

"What if Pam's had an accident and I didn't tell anyone she was still missing," Lizzy stared up at Jackson, her eyes filling with tears. "She could be laying in a ditch somewhere – she could...she could..."

Jackson put an arm around the girl's shoulders and told her to stop borrowing trouble. "Come on, we'll try phoning her first then, if we don't get any joy, we'll let

Chad know where we're going and then we'll take my car and go looking for her. Ok?"

Wiping the back of her hand over her watery eyes, Lizzy looked up at Jackson and nodded, so glad that he was around.

The office was empty when they got there so Jackson just used the phone to call Pam and waited for her to answer. When she didn't, he too became worried and frowned down at the desk so as to hide his expression from Lizzy. "No joy I'm afraid," he turned to the young girl and was met by Chad's stony face.

"What are you doing in here?" Chad's tone was none too friendly and when he shifted his eyes to Lizzy the girl quickly moved nearer to Jackson.

Seeing her fear spiked Jackson's protective instincts and his temper, though he managed to tame it so as not to frighten Lizzy further. "We're trying to contact Pam Hooper – she hasn't turned up as yet and we wanted to make sure she's ok."

"You wait till now to report your immediate supervisor absent?" Chad looked intently at Lizzy again then turned his gaze back to Jackson when the girl didn't answer.

"She told Matt first thing," Jackson defended, his spine stiffening. He didn't usually take against people but for Chad he'd make an exception.

"Do you have a car?" Chad asked without preamble, and Jackson nodded. "Good – there are two ways to get to Ivy Cottage – you take the village road and I'll go the long way round, we'll meet up at the cottage and see what we find."

"Y.you think s.something bad happened?" Lizzy's tiny voice asks nervously.

Realising that he'd frightened the girl silly didn't make Chad feel good and he managed a smile. "No, not really, but we have to check, right?"

Nodding, Lizzy actually managed to return his smile with a quivering one of her own.

"You wait here while we go take a look..." Chad told her and saw that Lizzy wanted to protest, "...we'll need someone to let us know if Pam turns up."

Looking up at Jackson, Lizzy watched him nod in agreement and heaved a sigh of capitulation. "Ok."

"That book Jackson used to find Pam's number..." and Chad pointed to the red book still open by the phone, "...has all the important numbers you're ever likely to need in it, including employees and emergency numbers."

"Ok," Lizzy said again, then looked up at Chad curiously. "Does that mean you're an employee just like me?"

That made Chad laugh out loud and Lizzy gulped then smiled nervously.

"I suppose I am," Chad agreed eventually. "The farm is Matt's now – I'm just visiting for a while."

"Oh." Lizzy looked so relieved that Chad let go another belt of laughter then waved over at Jackson.

"Come on, let's get going and find our wayward stable manager."

Although he'd told Lizzy that he didn't think anything bad had happened to Pam, Chad gave Jackson a meaningful look before getting into his car and told him to drive slow and keep his eyes peeled.

Chad turned his four by four left out of the farm gates and Jackson turned his old ford right towards the village.

Even going the long way round, Chad arrived at the cottage within ten minutes and found Jackson waiting for him. "Any sign?"

Shaking his head, Jackson looked concerned. "I've knocked on the door and she doesn't appear to be home. Do you know if she lives alone?"

Chad nodded and walked up to the front window to peer in. Cupping his hands on the window he leaned his face against them and studied the lounge in detail.

"Not a thing out of place," he murmured to himself. Turning back to Jackson, Chad's expression was openly worried. "This cottage used to belong to Pam's aunt — when she passed away she left it to Pam and she's lived here for the last couple of years."

"What about her parents?"

"They still live in the village," Chad informed him. "Passing property on to the next generation is often the only way to get them on the property ladder and keep them from moving away."

"Maybe we should take a look around back and then pay her parent's a visit if we don't find anything," Jackson suggested.

The two men negotiated the locked back gate to the side of the house and jumped down into the neatly kept back garden. Chad tried the back door but found it locked, then he rapped the door hard with his knuckles.

While Chad continued to rap on the back door Jackson moved to peer in the rear windows. The kitchen was so clean he was sure you could eat off the floor — not a cup or bowl was left on the side or in the sink. Then he looked in the breakfast room window and found the same level of tidiness there too.

"If I didn't know better, I'd say this cottage was unlived in," Jackson observed when Chad came to stand beside him, also looking through the cottage window.

"Hmm, either that or it's been recently vacated," Chad

mused, puzzling Pam's disappearance over in his mind.

"Maybe she went on holiday," Jackson suggested. "Hey, I didn't look to see if it was on the planner – did you?"

Frowning, Chad had to admit that he hadn't. "But you said the girl told Matt that Pam hadn't come in first thing this morning – surely he would have told her if Pam had merely gone on holiday."

"Yes..." Jackson agreed, "...although, Matt has had a lot on his mind lately, maybe he just forgot."

It was a possibility, but one Chad didn't put much hope in. "I'll drop in on the Hoopers – I've known them for years so it won't worry them if I turn up unexpected," he explained when Jackson turned to him.

"Ok, I'll get back to the farm – you'll let us know as soon as you do, right?" Jackson demanded evenly. "Lizzy is worried as hell."

"I'll do that."

CHAPTER THIRTEEN

"What do you mean, she's missing?" I demanded when Chad drove over to the top most field to let me know that Pam was nowhere to be found.

"I mean, Jackson and I called at the house, searched the roads between here and there, and I called in to see John and Isabelle — they complained that Pam hadn't been by over the weekend — something she never misses doing normally," Chad recounted soberly.

Mac switched off the grain trailer and came to stand alongside the two men, just in case they came to blows again. "Everything ok?"

"No it bloody isn't," I exploded, now just as worried as Lizzy had been. "Pam seems to have disappeared off the face of the earth according to Chad!"

A bad feeling crept through Mac's bones. He didn't

like Doom Sayers who seemed to revel in the misfortune of others, but if there was a possibility that Theodore Swain was involved in any way...well...

"When did you last speak to Pam?" Mac asked, looking from me to Chad.

"I don't really know..." Chad frowned thoughtfully, "...probably Thursday or Friday just gone."

"Friday," I stated more confidently. "She was fine. She gave Lizzy a riding lesson and had some more planned for that morning – there was nothing unusual about her."

"So you saw her in the morning – what about the afternoon?" Mac pressed for more details.

"Actually, yes, I saw Pam just as she was knocking off around 4 – said she was going to give Lizzy a lift home then go into the village for a bit of shopping," I recalled. "You know we don't clock in or out exactly on time and Pam is always putting in extra hours," I told Chad when I noticed my brother's frown.

"Yes, yes," Chad waved that concern away. "But who would she have seen over the weekend, do you know?"

At any other time I would have been reluctant to say, but Pam was missing and Fallon might know where she went. "I know she was planning to meet up with Fallon – girl talk," I added when Chad turned to glare at me.

"And I would be the topic of conversation no doubt," Chad ground out angrily.

Before things could get out of hand, Mac jumped in and got our attention focused back on Pam. "I think we all agree that Pam is the main concern right now. Perhaps one of you should speak to Fallon or Wesley – maybe Pam is there right now?"

I didn't really think so but it was possible that one of them might know where Pam had gone.

"I'll go," Chad offered, surprising me and I lifted a brow. "You have enough to do here."

And I did. I still had one and a half large fields of wheat to harvest and 8 hectares of maize to bring in after that. It was all well and good having the largest farm in the district but it took a lot of work to keep it working efficiently.

"If you're sure," I offered, knowing that the visit to the Craemer's might be an uncomfortable one.

"No problem," Chad assured me before striding back to his car.

I watched my brother go and had to force myself to climb back up into the cab of the combine harvester.

Damn it, Pam, where the hell are you?

Jackson was helping Lizzy in the stables, mainly keeping her occupied so that she didn't have time to worry about Pam. At least, that was the idea but he could see that it wasn't always working.

"I'll help you take the horses out to the paddock, that'll give us a clear run to get the stalls mucked out," Jackson told Lizzy.

"You're going to help me?" Lizzy was stunned but relieved to hear that Jackson would be around for a while longer.

"We'll help each other," Jackson smiled. "I'll help you with the stalls and you can help me to check on the live stock and make sure they've got enough feed and the water troughs are full."

"I will," Lizzy agreed eagerly, her eyes as round as saucers.

For the next couple of hours Lizzy and Jackson worked mainly in the stable yard and got all of the immediate work done. But every now and then he'd catch Lizzy gazing off towards the main house obviously still worrying about Pam.

"Ok, we're done here, now it's your turn to help me out," Jackson sighed, happy with what they'd managed to get done. "Do you know if Pam had any riding lessons booked in?" he asked Lizzy as they headed off.

"Not this morning..." Lizzy informed him, "...but she has a couple of one-to-ones booked in for this afternoon."

"Well, hopefully Pam will be in by then but if not we'll need to phone and cancel."

I managed to continue working until we'd finished harvesting the wheat fields, but I refused to continue with the Maize crop.

"I'm calling it a day," I told Mac, who wasn't really surprised. "I can't just carry on like nothing's happened. If Chad had found her he'd have either called me or been back by now." And I took out my mobile to check I hadn't missed any calls. But I hadn't.

"What are you planning to do?" Mac asked.

"Well, the last thing we know for sure is that Pam was planning to go into the village for some shopping – I'll start there and see where it leads me."

Mac nodded, it didn't sound like Matt could get into too much trouble just asking a few questions but he offered to tag along just in case.

"No, I'll be ok – you and Jackson keep an eye on Lizzy and leave Pam to me and Chad," I instructed. "Will you make sure she gets some lunch and a ride home if I'm not back in time to take her?"

"No problem – we'll see to Lizzy."

They all had their suspicions that she didn't have a very good home life and it made them all the more protective of Lizzy.

"If you could give me a ride back to the house I'll get changed and get off."

But once changed I hadn't headed straight for the village. Instead I'd driven the lanes to Ivy cottage, going the long way round first and then taking the shorter route towards the village. I just needed to be sure that Pam's car wasn't in some ditch – it was all well and good Chad and Jackson saying they'd checked but I had to do it for myself.

Christ, Pam...this isn't like you! I've never known you to let anyone down, let alone just disappear without a word.

Going first to the small supermarket, I asked a couple of the local girls if Pam had been in last Friday or any time since.

Stacy remembered Pam doing some shopping on the Friday but hadn't seen her when she'd been working the tills again on Saturday morning. "But that isn't unusual..." Stacy informed me, "...it's rare for Pam to come in on a Saturday; she's usually doing stuff for John and Isabelle. Sometimes comes in on a Wednesday, but that's about it."

"When you saw her on Friday, was she with anyone?"

The girl frowned thoughtfully. "No, not in the shop anyway."

"Not in the shop – did you see her with someone outside?" I asked, and looked up and through the large glass windows to the village streets.

"Yes, she was chatting to that rich bloke who bought the old Henry farm." Then Stacy scoffed derisively, "Not that he's ever farmed it – I hear he all but tore the old house down and built some fancy new place instead. He's even got a helicopter according to Helen," and the girl lifted her chin to indicate the girl on the next till.

"He has..." Helen declared having overheard the conversation, "...I saw it take off one time when I was on the way home. Scared your cattle when he flew low over your farm," she informed me, her expression disapproving.

"Did he now!"

"Yep, they was running from the road side of the field and off to the other side – I stopped to watch in case any of them got hurt, but they seemed ok once the helicopter was gone so I just went home," Helen recounted solemnly.

"Thanks for that." I gave her a smile and Helen lit up like a Christmas tree. "I'll have a word with Mr Swain... make sure he doesn't do that again."

Looking pleased with herself, Helen turned back to her till and served the next customer.

"Thanks for the info – I'll buy you a drink next time I see you in the Rose & Crown," I offered and waved them goodbye.

So, Swain is possibly involved — but I'll ask a few more questions in case Pam was seen with anyone else.

After the supermarket, I went to the butcher's shop, and a little greengrocery, but they just confirmed what Stacy had said.

Thinking I wouldn't get any more information from the village, I walked towards my car but felt someone tug on my arm and stopped.

"She was in tears," the middle aged woman told me when I turned around to face her.

"Mrs Coates, you saw Pam Hooper?"

"I did..." the widower told him, "...and she looked like she'd been given some really bad news. Saw that Mr Swain when he walked away from her too — he didn't look unhappy at all. In fact, I'd say he couldn't have looked happier if he'd won the lottery."

"So you think it was something he said that made Pam cry?" I asked, already suspecting the answer.

"It definitely was," Mrs Coates crossed her arms under her ample breasts. "I spoke to Pam not five minutes before that man showed up — she was happy as Larry, not a care in the world that I could see."

"Thanks, Mrs Coates, you take care now and tell Pam to get in touch if you run into her before I do, ok?"

"I will." Mrs Coates raised a hand in farewell and

headed back in the direction she'd come from.

There's something really weird about this. Pam wouldn't have left of her own volition without at least contacting her parents – or me, for that matter. It just isn't the way she's wired!

On the way back to Langdon Farm, I decided to take a detour and pulled into the Swain driveway, stopping in front of the house.

I'd barely gotten out of the car before Fenella came rushing out. "Matt..." she smiled happily, her arms held out wide, "...I was beginning to think you'd dumped me."

I didn't stop her from flinging her arms about my neck and giving me a hug, but when Fenella moved in for a kiss I moved away.

"I need to see your father, is he in?"

Looking anything but happy now, Fenella frowned and shook her head. "He's at the paper," she snapped turning back to the house then changed her mind and stomped back to where I still stood. "You didn't even come to see me, did you?"

"Not this time." I tried to smile to soften the blow to her ego but she could tell I was forcing it and began having a tantrum.

This was the old Fenella, the demanding young woman who always wanted her way. "Not any time, as far as I can tell. You have all the passion of a damp squid — why did you ever ask me out if you didn't want to be with me?"

I almost expected her to finish by stamping her foot, but Fenella suddenly calmed and looked genuinely hurt.

I could deal with her temper and her tantrums, but this hurt look made me feel like a heel.

"I'm sorry, it seemed like a good idea at the time, and I never meant to hurt you," I tried to explain.

With her lower lip trembling, Fenella looked up at me wearing her heart plainly on her sleeve. "You really have no idea," she told me, shaking her head in wonder. "I've been in love with you for the longest time — but you've never felt the same, have you?"

Even though I could see the tears teetering in her eyes, I couldn't lie to her anymore. "I'm sorry. You're a gorgeous woman with a lot to offer any man-"

"Just not you!" Fenella interrupted, her temper rising again. "So why did you ask me out, was it a bet with someone in the village?" Then her eyes went wide and she looked like the penny had dropped with a clatter to the bottom of her broken heart. "That's it, isn't it — you did it for a bet — a bet with Wesley Craemer!"

Her voice was barely more than a whisper, its tone appalled and full of shame.

"No!" I stepped forward putting my hands on her

arms and giving Fenella a gentle shake. "I would never do a thing like that — how could you think it!"

"Then why?" The tears were falling now, her simple question the undoing of him.

"Fenella..." I began softly, but realised that what I'd agreed to with her father amounted to much the same thing. I had felt like the victim in all this, bought as a plaything for the spoiled rich daughter of the house. Yet there Fenella stood, heartbroken and clearly hurting. "You deserve much better than me," I told her sincerely, touching a hand to her damp cheek. "I've been a complete fool, but I would never hurt you intentionally. I just hope that one day you will find it in your heart to forgive me."

I turned away, returning to my car and climbed inside without looking back at Fenella.

Her father should be publicly flogged for what he's done — to Fenella and to me! And what did he have to do with Pam's disappearance — because I know he had something to do with it!

Unable to bear going straight back to the farm, I drove to Ivy cottage again, the need to see Pam a desperate one now.

The moment I pulled up on the drive, however, I knew that the little house was empty. *It's like she was never here. But she was, and she will be again!*

CHAPTER FOURTEEN

"You're the one who told me that Swain was dangerous, now you think I'm deranged because I finally believe it," I paced the living room, glaring at Chad.

"I just think you're allowing your emotions to rule your head!" Chad was tied in so many knots over Fallon he didn't know what to make of Pam's disappearance. Although he knew Swain to be a very dangerous, shady character, he wasn't sure that he was actually capable of 'getting rid' of someone. "Fallon seems to think Pam may have taken off to put some space between you two – apparently she was pretty upset when they last spoke."

"So that's it?! You expect me to just sit back and wait for Pam to show up again?" I was beyond disbelief, I was astounded to think that Pam might be being held somewhere against her will and my brother expected me to do nothing about it.

Frowning up at me, Chad knew that if he were in my shoes he wouldn't be able to sit back and wait either. "The only other option is to go to the police – but I can't see them doing much as there's no proof that Pam didn't leave of her own free will."

"Well, at least I can pay Swain back what I owe him," I ground out with some small satisfaction. "We finally got our invoices paid – though why it took them so long in the first place is still a mystery. None of them have ever delayed payment like that before!"

"Does that mean you won't be going ahead with the building project?" Chad asked curiously.

He'd already told me that he didn't want a share of the profits from the project – but what he hadn't told me was why he didn't need it.

"No, I'm still going to build the affordable housing – this village needs it and we don't need the land to continue farming the way we always have," I declared firmly. "As to the police – I think I'll run that idea past Mr and Mrs Hooper first. With any luck they'll have heard from Pam if she really is ok."

"And what are you going to do about Fenella Swain – her father won't just let you pay him back and walk away," Chad reminded me, concerned that I might end up getting my legs broken...or worse.

"Really!" I snarled, actually looking forward to telling Theodore Swain what I thought of him. "I doubt he'd want his daughter to know the kind of lengths he was prepared to go to in order to buy her the husband she wanted – do you?"

One brow raised, Chad looked up at me with something akin to admiration in his eyes. "And that's what you intend to tell Swain?" When I nodded, Chad let out a whistle then sat back in his chair considering me. "You know what, you might just be right. Swain is a bully, he relies on the little man being too scared to stand up to him – maybe you can teach him a lesson in good manners, bro!"

The two brothers were still laughing when Jackson walked into the sitting room, having knocked on the door first. "Sorry to disturb you but I think you need to come and see this."

"What's wrong – is it the cattle, the machinery, what?" I asked already following Jackson out of the house and, surprisingly, round to the stables. "Oh Christ – tell me Lizzy didn't go into Ronan's stall?!"

"You'd think she had to look at her," Jackson stopped, frowning heavily, and pointed to Symphony's stall where Lizzy was already mucking out. "She said she walked into a door – but I'd like to know what kind of door caused bruises on her arms and legs as well as giving her a fucking shiner!

"Jesus!" We had always suspected that Lizzy's home life was less than happy, but I'd never dreamed it might also be violent. "I wish Pam were here, Lizzy would probably open up to her."

"Well she isn't and we can't let this carry on," Jackson asserted firmly. "She's no more than skin and bone as it is – it's a wonder he didn't break any of them as battered as Lizzy looks!"

Christ, can this day get any worse!

Walking quietly into Symphony's stall, I watched Lizzy working like nothing was wrong. Apart from the odd groan or grimace, she didn't slow down at all.

"Oh! You scared me half to death," Lizzy dropped the rake and stood with both hands clapped over her heart.

"Looks like someone beat me to it..." I glared at the bright bruises that stood out from her pale skin, "...and I want to know who it was." But I could see it in her eyes, even before she spoke, that she was going to try to fob me off with the same story she'd told Jackson. "You lie to me, Lizzy, you walk – do you get that?!"

Suddenly Lizzy was on her knees, pleading with me not to sack her. "I can still do my work – please Mr Langdon..." she cried, reverting back to my formal title,

"...I love it here – I'll do extra hours to make up for being slow – I'll learn to ride on my own time and-"

"Get up, for christ's sake!" I tried not to sound angry, Lizzy didn't need frightening any more than she already had been. "The only thing I want from you is the truth – your work has always been exemplary. Now spill!"

Without a moment's hesitation, Lizzy spilled the whole sorry tale. "It's just that the kids get a bit noisy now and then and it's my job to keep them quiet - dad works shifts and it drives him insane when they wake him up before its time."

"What about your mother, where was she?"

"Mam watches the kids in the week – she says it wouldn't pay her to work as she'd have to pay to get the kids minded. But at weekends I take my turn to watch them and mam works at the supermarket in the village," Lizzy stated matter of fact.

"And those bruises are the thanks you get?" I shook my head in despair then took Lizzy carefully by the elbow so as not to hurt her further. "Come with me – I should take you to the doctor but I've got a feeling you would refuse."

Chewing nervously on her bottom lip, Lizzy nodded.

"Thought so – but we can at least put some salve on those bruises – your eye's going to take some time to go down," I observed, holding the front door of the house open for Lizzy, and followed her in. "My mother always used ice when Chad blacked my eye," I told her to distract Lizzy's attention. But when she gasped I laughed and said, "I got my own back often enough – but this kind of violence is something else." I put a gentle hand under Lizzy's chin to tip her face up to the light.

"What the hell?!"

It was Chad, he'd been upstairs but had come down to find out what the crisis had been and had walked into the kitchen to find me examining Lizzy's swollen eye.

Always nervous around Chad, Lizzy took a step back.

"Don't do that – I don't hit little girls," he told her, but kept his tone deliberately gentle. "You're dad do that?"

Too scared to lie, Lizzy silently nodded her head then watched as Chad turned around and left.

"Is he angry with me?" she asked, unsure of what had just happened.

"No, Lizzy – but he's angry at someone." And I just hoped that my brother would calm down a bit before he found Lizzy's father.

"Ok, hold this bag of ice against your eye and I'll put some salve on your arms and legs," I told her, squeezing the tube of ointment and very gently smoothing it over her bruises with the tip of a finger.

Apart from the odd wince, Lizzy bore up to it stoically.

"You really aren't going to sack me?" Lizzy asked quietly.

"You haven't done anything wrong so why would I sack you?" My heart ached when she smiled so brightly in spite of her injuries.

"Thanks, Matt."

"So, I'm back to being Matt — that must mean we're friends again, right?"

Lizzy nodded shyly - she liked Matt so much, he was like the big brother she'd always longed for — someone who would have stood up to her father when he got mad.

"Ok, that's about the best we can do — let me see the eye," I told her and winced when she lifted the bag of ice. "Nothing heavy for you today. I'll do the mucking out and you clean the tack — there's a couple of saddles that need a good going over — Mac will show you how it's done. Ok?"

But Lizzy shook her head, "Mucking out is my job, if I don't do my work Pam will think I'm not up to it."

"Pam wouldn't think like that at all, not if I explained," I told her firmly. "And I'm the boss around here — if I say you clean tack then you clean tack...got it?"

"Got it." Lizzy groaned, none too happy to have her duties taken away from her.

"You'll be shovelling horse muck again soon enough — anyone else would be glad of a break from it," I told her, and rolled my eyes in comic emphasis.

I got the laughter that I'd hoped for and felt easier for knowing that Lizzy didn't seem to have come to any real harm. But if she turned up to work looking like that again...

I had to push down the anger that wanted to meet out punishment on a man who could inflict this kind of injury on his own daughter — but I had a feeling Chad might already be doing it for me.

"You let me know when you've had enough," I told Lizzy as I walked her back to the stable yard. "I'll drive you home and pick you up in the morning."

I knew that Pam usually gave the girl a ride home, but Lizzy had always insisted on walking to work in the mornings. I had a feeling it was to do with her 'duties' at home, but I wouldn't be taking no for an answer from now on.

"I can do my hours," Lizzy proclaimed proudly. "I don't shirk off work, not for anything."

I had to admire her spirit, but I was more glad than I'd ever let on when I saw Mac in the tack room, getting down a saddle to work on. "Hi, you have a helper today," I told Mac, and noticed that the older man didn't seem surprised by Lizzy's colourful appearance. *Jackson must have filled him in.*

"I want Lizzy to learn how to clean a saddle – she can do the other tack on her own, but she hasn't had a go at a saddle yet," I smiled encouragingly at Lizzy.

As I walked away, I could hear Mac's kindly voice explaining what to use where and how to get the best results. *Good old Mac, he'll take Lizzy under his wing and make sure she doesn't over do it. I'll nip back later to see if she needs to go home early – though I'm not sure that would be a safe option. What the hell am I supposed to do now – I can't just send her home to get beaten again.*

Lizzy was true to her word, however, and managed to stay the entire day with Mac watching over her to make sure she didn't do anything strenuous.

Chad had phoned, mid afternoon, to say that he'd 'had a word with Stan Collier', Lizzy's father, and that the man wouldn't be laying hands on his daughter again any time soon.

Whatever the hell that means – but I'm glad to know that Lizzy should be safe to go home.

Even so, I walked Lizzy to the door when I took her home and waited for it to be opened.

It was her father who opened it, and he looked warily at me as he waved Lizzy inside.

"I gather my brother was here earlier," I said, my voice low so as not to be overheard. When Stan Collier nodded in confirmation, I moved just a step closer and said, "Whatever he said goes double for me. If I see one hair on Lizzy's head out of place you'll wish you'd never been born!"

A small, pudgy man, Stan wasn't the least bit brave — unless the person he was standing up to was even smaller than him, as Lizzy was.

The door closed in my face, but not before the ruddy cheeked man had given me a brief nod.

Yeah, that's what I thought! You miserable little excuse of a man!

About to get back into my car, I stopped to answer my mobile. "Hey, Wes, what's up?"

"Chad is what's up," Wes replied, sounding as if he was struggling with something. "I came here for a quiet pint before going home but your brother seems to have been here for quite some time already."

"Chad? Is that him I can hear in the background?"

"That's him alright," Wes confirmed. "Thinks he's god's gift to women right now — he stinks like he drank the sodding brewery dry!"

"Hey, ladies, how about coming out to dinner with me and my friend," Chad shouted across the car park of the

Rose & Crown pub, then belched loudly. "Oops, sorry about that – probably should have had something to eat before the beer, hey." And he laughed so hard he almost toppled Wes over when he doubled up.

"Good lord – I can't remember the last time Chad tied one on," I laughed, shaking my head as I listened to the girl's haughty reply to my brother's offer.

"Stop laughing and get your arse down here," Wes demanded, obviously struggling to hold onto his phone.

"As it happens I'm not far away – I'll see you in a couple of minutes."

Chad looked every bit as bad as I had envisioned. Wes had hold of him around the waist and had one of Chad's arms draped across his shoulders – but Chad was legless, his knees buckling at each attempted step.

"What the hell...why did Shirley keep serving him when he was in this state?!" I didn't find it so funny now that I could see how bad my brother was.

"To be fair, he wasn't this bad until he got outside, then the air hit him and-" Wes jumped back a step just in time to save his shoes – Chad had emptied the contents of his stomach at his feet. "Shit!"

"Damn it, Chad – don't you do that in my car," I snapped as I took hold of my brother on the opposite side to Wes.

But Chad was no longer listening; he was out cold on his feet.

"What brought this on, do you know?" I asked Wes as we struggled to get Chad into the back of my car and do his seatbelt up.

"I don't know what's going on between him and my sister, but I have an idea that might be what's behind this," Wes told me, shutting the car door on Chad. "Fallon's been in a foul mood since he left..." and Wes jerked a thumb in Chad's direction, "...now he's back she's worse than ever – more so since he came over the other night."

"Oh." I rubbed a hand on the back of my neck, a guilty feeling making me feel awkward. "I suppose I should have come over – I did offer..." I added when Wes gave me a wry look, "...but you know how pig-headed my brother can be, and he probably thought it was a good excuse to come over and speak to Fallon."

Remembering the reason for Chad's visit, Wes asked if I'd heard from Pam yet.

"No," I replied flatly. "I want to go to the police, but what the hell do I tell them? I suspect a prominent citizen in our little community is a gangster and has done away with my girlfriend," I scoffed, and laughed bitterly at the thought. "Chad's right, I have no proof of wrong doing –

Pam may have taken off of her own free will. And who could blame her?"

"Girlfriend?" Wes raised a curious brow.

"Well she will be, if I ever find her," I frowned.

"And what does Fenella Swain think of that idea?" Wes asked, confused by the turn of events.

I shuffled my feet, uncomfortable at the memory of Fenella in tears. "She was upset when I broke it off – but she has a right to real happiness, not some facsimile of it that her daddy bought for her!"

"You didn't tell her that?!" Wes asked, astounded.

"Of course I didn't – I'm not that heartless," I told him. "Though I nearly did – she thought I'd asked her out for a bet with you, but I soon dissuaded her of that idea," I added quickly when Wesley's sharp eyes bored into me.

"I should hope you did. But what about Mr Swain – how did he take the breakup?"

"I have no idea," I had to admit. "I haven't had the pleasure of hearing from him as yet. Though I'm sure it won't be long before I do!"

CHAPTER FIFTEEN

When Chad woke up the next morning he couldn't remember much about the day before. He'd gone to the Rose & Crown just to get off the farm and away from people for a while – he'd needed time to think.

Good christ! He grasped his throbbing head between his hands as he got out of the bed and then had to put a hand to the nearest wall to stop it swaying. *Oh shit!*

He made it to the bathroom just in time.

"I'm surprised you've got anything left in your gut to throw up," I told my brother when Chad managed to raise his head out of the loo.

"How did I get home – I didn't drive did I?" Chad looked up at me with worried eyes.

"No; Wes called me and we both got you into my car. He followed us home and helped me carry you up to bed," I informed Chad, quirking an eyebrow up when my brother turned around and sat on the loo.

He was stark naked, but Chad had no shame when he was in this state. "Thanks."

Deciding that was about all I could expect from Chad for now, I waited patiently then helped my brother back to his bedroom.

"I'll bring you some coffee up," I offered when Chad slumped down to sit on his bed. "A good strong mug of black coffee should wake a few brain cells up at least."

Chad didn't answer – just barely nodded his aching head and lifted a hand in acknowledgement, letting it fall back heavily to his knees.

Having given Chad his coffee, I was back downstairs and sitting at the large kitchen table looking out over the back yard.

I need to man up and go speak to Theodore Swain. It won't be pretty, but at least I won't have it hanging over me like a guillotine blade about to fall. And I need to pay him the loan back – now that we've been paid up to date I don't need his money.

Which is what I tried to explain at the bank in the first place – it was only ever a short-term problem.

Before I could set off, however, I got a surprise call from Ashton. "Hey sis, it's great to hear from you. I've been told you're doing some amazing things in the big world of show jumping."

"I'll give you 'hey sis'," Ashton growled down the phone. "What the heck have you been up to – I just heard that you got engaged to Fenella Swain. Are you completely nuts?!"

Holding my mobile away from my ear, I could still hear every word my sister yelled. "Calm down, you've got it all wrong," I told her quickly before Ashton could have another go. "I took her out a few times – we are not engaged, nor do we have any intention of becoming engaged. Where did you hear that, anyway?"

"Never you mind where I heard it, but it was from a very reliable source," Ashton assured me, still seething.

"Can't be that reliable, it isn't true," I stated firmly. "By the way, you haven't heard anything from Pam, have you? She seems to have disappeared – I'm really worried about her."

A loud disbelieving huff was her first reply, then Ashton told him that she was glad if Pam had dumped him.

"I didn't say she'd dumped me," I challenged feeling aggrieved. "She didn't even have the courtesy to tell me she was leaving, let alone that she was dumping me!"

"And can you blame her?!" Ashton screeched at me. "You lead her on, all these years, then you start taking that rich brat out right in front of her eyes. Personally, I'd have decked you before I left!"

"I wish she had," I admitted quietly. "I did something so stupid, but I'm about to set that right. I'm not with Fenella anymore..." I explained dully, "...I never really was but I don't know where Pam is to tell her."

"And you expect her to just take you back?" Ashton asked, somewhat incredulous.

"We were never together officially," I defended weakly. "But I admit, we were working our way up to it – then I messed things up and couldn't get myself out of it."

Hearing his misery softened Ashton's ire. "I don't know what you did or what's going on but the source was Theodore Swain," she told me, deciding that I needed to know. "He told Pa- people..." Ashton caught herself just in time, almost letting Pam's secret out of the bag, "... that you were about to announce your engagement to his daughter."

"That's ridiculous," I blustered, stunned to think that Swain had gone that far.

"According to him, the wedding will be some time next year," Ashton informed me, not quite so angrily now that she knew the announcement to be untrue.

Rubbing the back of my neck, I tried to think what I could do to put things right. "I need to find Pam – make sure she's alright and explain what happened. I just hope I haven't lost her for good."

Sorely tempted to put him out of his misery, Ashton brought the conversation to an end before she caved. "I can tell you that she's safe, but that's all I can tell you."

"What, you've spoken to her?"

"I have – now don't ask me any more – I promised I wouldn't tell you anything," Ashton explained, feeling wretched.

"Ok, I get it. But if she calls again..." I fell silent, unable to get the words out.

"I'll tell her you know you were a jerk and that you need to speak to her," Ashton filled in for me.

"Yes. Please."

The call ended and I didn't know how to feel. I was angry with Theo Swain and I was still annoyed with Pam for leaving without a word. But now that I knew what Swain was putting about I couldn't really blame her.

I should knock the arrogant bastard's head off for this, but I'll settle for giving Swain his money back and getting him out of my life!

I didn't bother to write a cheque – I didn't want to give Swain the chance to rip it up in my face. Instead, I went into the village and withdrew the cash from the bank then took a chance on Swain being home and drove to his house.

I could see the large Mercedes Theodore Swain drove

still parked at the side of the house — but I also knew that he sometimes used his helicopter for getting into work.

Giving the front door a firm knock, I waited for it to be opened. I wasn't the least bit nervous; adrenaline was fuelling my anger which blocked out everything else.

It was Molly who opened the door — she looked a bit surprised to see me but, never-the-less, asked me inside.

"I was hoping to speak to Mr Swain," I explained once the front door had been closed behind me. "Is he home?"

Looking decidedly nervous, Molly nodded and whispered, "He's in a terrible mood — are you sure you wouldn't rather come back another day?"

So, Fenella has told him that we're no longer an item — well, that's just as it should be!

"No, Molly; if Mr Swain can see me I'd rather get this over with," I told her with a smile of thanks.

Looking like she didn't envy me, Molly asked me to wait just a minute and she'd find out if Mr Swain was free to see me.

In the event I didn't need Molly to tell me that Theodore Swain was available, I could hear him for myself.

"Get him in here, now!" Theodore Swain bellowed like a grizzly bear woken out of hibernation.

Walking to the office, I met up with a pale faced Molly

and patted her shoulder in reassurance as I stepped past her into Swain's office.

I managed to close the door before the shouting started; when it continued I pulled up a chair and sat myself down...and waited.

For several minutes Theo told me what an ingrate I was, a double dealing swindler and all sorts of other colourful descriptives.

"Have you got nothing to say in your own defence?" Theodore finally asked when I remained silent.

"As a matter of fact, I do." I got unhurriedly to my feet and stood almost toe-to-toe with Theo. "Your daughter is one of the most decent women I've ever had the pleasure of getting to know - apart from when she's throwing a tantrum to get her own way, that is. And I have to wonder – I've only met Mrs Swain a few times but she must be a saint to remain married to you and to pass on such admirable traits as Fenella has that you have no hope of ever possessing."

"Why you-" Theo swung a fist upwards and towards my face, but I caught it easily and gave it a crushing squeeze.

"I would just love to take you on..." I growled, my face contorted with anger, "...but I've hurt Fenella enough because of you – now sit the fuck down!"

I pushed Theo away from me and kept watchful eyes on the man until he'd taken his seat.

Getting out an envelope, I pushed it across the large desk and watched while Theo looked at it hesitantly.

"What's this?" Theo asked, but I had an idea that he already knew.

"Open it and see," I told him.

Theo undid the envelope and took a look inside then threw it back across the desk towards me. "You don't get out of our agreement that easily – we made a bargain and you will keep your end of it!"

"Or what?" I asked, truly intrigued to know how Swain intended to force me to comply.

"Or you, and your family, will suffer the consequences," Theo threatened, his expression stony hard.

"You can't hurt me or my family," I told him, not entirely convinced that it was true. "I've given you what you're owed plus interest at the going rate – we have nothing more to say."

I turned and opened the office door before Theo deigned to reply. "Arranging a few late payments and a refusal for a bank loan were nothing..." he sneered as I turned back to look at him, "...I'll bring you and your family down to gutter level and then buy your farm out from under you! You know I can do it," Theo stared, challenging me to deny it.

"I know you're an evil bastard and Fenella would be better off without you," I replied sternly. "I hope to God she meets someone wonderful who will take care of her and get her out of your treacherous clutches!"

With that I turned to leave, running smack into a very pale looking Fenella.

"I'm sorry you overheard that..." I told her, putting a gentle hand to her cheek, "...but maybe it's better that you know. Take care, Fenella."

CHAPTER SIXTEEN

For the next couple of days, I worked like the devil himself was at my heels. Harvesting was going really well with me, Mac and Jackson putting in so many long hard hours.

Chad had tried to talk to me on my return from the Swain place, but I had brushed the incident aside and hadn't shared what had been said with anyone.

It was late, nearly 10 o'clock at night, when a strong knock came at the front door. Chad began to rise from his seat but I waved him back and went instead.

There was a muffled conversation and then the voices got louder - so loud that Chad came out of the sitting room to see what was going on.

"What the hell?!"

"Call our solicitor," I shouted over my shoulder as I

was being hustled out of my own house. "This is Swain's doing – just get Ferguson down to the station as soon as you can!"

Watching, stunned, as his brother was being manhandled into a police car, Chad took a moment to move. Then he ran for his mobile, found Ferguson's number and dialled it.

An hour later and Chad was pacing the front office of the local police station. It wasn't large, just an out posting of the main station in Upper Stanton, the nearest large town.

He'd managed to get a quick word with the solicitor before he'd been shown through to the holding cells where Matt was being held. It hadn't been a fruitful conversation; the solicitor seemed as oblivious of the charges being brought against his brother as Chad was.

Unable to bear the confines of the small building, Chad eventually went outside where he continued his pacing.

This doesn't make any sense! What could Swain have pinned on him to get the police to actually arrest Matt? He told me he went over to pay Swain back the money he borrowed – maybe Swain is trying to say that he stole something while he was there?

No, that wouldn't be reason enough to drag someone

out of their home in handcuffs. It would have to be something pretty bad for that. Unless he was trying to say it was something really valuable. But if he was talking with Swain, when would he have had the opportunity?

Blowing out a frustrated breath, Chad decided to go back inside the station and walked up to the front desk.

"When can I see my brother?" he asked tersely. "You've had Matt locked up for hours – I want to make sure he's alright!"

The officer manning the desk gave Chad a pitying look – he'd known both men since their school days together. "Look, Chad, he's got his solicitor with him – that's the best we can do for now."

"But I don't even know what you're accusing him of," Chad raged quietly. "If your Joe was in here you'd be doing exactly the same as I'm doing, so help me will you?"

Officer David Brent looked full of sympathy, but had to shake his head. "I can't, Chad – I would if I could, but I can't."

Nodding his head in resignation, Chad took a seat and waited. Ten minutes later Ferguson came out to him, looking anything but reassuring.

Taking Chad by the elbow, Ferguson encouraged Chad out of the station doors to the night air. "He's been charged with murder," the solicitor told him, sighing heavily as he delivered the terrible news.

"What?!" It wasn't a question that exploded from Chad, but an exclamation of disbelief. "Matthias isn't capable of murder – you know that, right?"

The solicitor looked guarded, but nodded his head in agreement. "The problem is, Matthias knew the girl, even dated her for a while."

"Not Fenella Swain...?" Chad felt like he'd been pole axed, even when he saw Ferguson shake his head.

"No, it was her best friend, Camille Parsons," the solicitor told him, regret sounding heavy in his tired voice. "I've known the Parsons almost as long as I've know your family..." he recalled sadly, "...I can't imagine what they're going through, poor souls."

"Camille Parsons? Camille Parsons?" Chad repeated as though he had to convince himself he'd heard correctly.

"Yes, I'm afraid so, and your brother has no alibi for the night in question," Ferguson confirmed.

"And you're just going to let it go at that?!" Chad demanded angrily. "You're going to let them keep him in a cage just because no one can verify his whereabouts – that probably puts half the men in Dersley Dale under suspicion!"

"Maybe so, but only your brother is known to have dated Camille Parsons and also Pamela Hooper." Ferguson watched Chad closely as he gave him this information.

"Pam – what the hell has she-" Losing all colour from his face, Chad became very still. "Please don't tell me they found her body too?"

"No, but she has been missing for a while now and the police seem convinced that she has met with the same end as Camille," Ferguson explains.

This was a nightmare of the worst kind – one Chad knew he couldn't wake up from.

"What the hell do we do now?" Chad asked, a hand pressing against his throbbing brow.

"Well...the reappearance of Pamela Hooper would be a great start," Ferguson mused. "It would look a great deal better for Matthias if two of his girlfriends were not thought to be dead – it forms a pattern in the minds of the police."

"But there's no proof that Pam is dead," Chad argued.

"There's no proof that she is alive, either," Ferguson reminded Chad gently.

"Then we have to find her."

Sitting in his cell, Matt couldn't take it all in. He'd been arrested for murder, Camille Parsons was dead – had been murdered and Pam was still missing.

Pushing a hand back through my overlong hair, I got up to pace the tiny room.

I don't know how, but this has to be connected to Swain! He said he'd bring me and my family down and this will do it big time. But how...did he actually have Camille murdered just to put me where I am now? Even I can't believe he'd go that far.

But what if he did? What if he hired someone to do it – oh god...does that mean he's done away with Pam too? Is it just a matter of time before her body is found?

The following morning Chad tried desperately to locate Pamela Hooper by calling all the people he knew in the village and surrounding areas. Having got no joy doing that, he then called a detective agency and demanded that someone be sent out to see him immediately.

"I'll pay double your going rate for your top investigator," Chad told the manager he'd insisted on being put through to. "My brother has been arrested for something he didn't do, but we can't prove that without locating Pamela Hooper!"

Assured that their top investigator would get to him within the hour, Chad finally began to feel like he was doing something positive.

Going out to find Mac and Jackson, Chad went to the main barn then round to the stable yard. "Mac..." he shouted over to the older man, "...I want to speak to all of you, get Jackson and Lizzy and come up to the house."

Watching Chad stride away, Mac didn't like the feeling of impending doom that had just settled over him.

Going into a nearby stall, Mac told Lizzy to drop what she was doing and come with him. "We need to find Jackson and go up to the house – Chad wants a word with all of us."

Lizzy looked scared – even though she now knew that it was Chad who had threatened her father if he ever hurt her again, she was still very nervous around him.

"What did we do wrong?" Lizzy asked as she trotted alongside Mac. "He wouldn't fire us all," she speculated hopefully.

"I don't believe it's anything like that," Mac assured her gently. "But I don't think it's going to be good news either."

Rounding the corner to the paddock, Mac spied Jackson turning Ronan out for some exercise.

"Jackson..." Mac called out to his son, "...we're needed up at the house. Now," he added when Jackson waved a casual hand to him then stood watching Ronan kick up his hooves.

"What's the emergency?" Jackson frowned at his father as he joined him and Lizzy after fastening the paddock gate behind him.

"We don't know..." Lizzy chimed in before Mac could

answer, "...Chad just told Mac to get us up to the house."

"You think it's serious?" Jackson looked at his father for a clue to what was going on.

"I don't know any more than you two," Mac told them as they approached the front door of the house and went inside.

"In here," Chad called out from the sitting room. And when they'd all filed in he told them to take a seat. "You might be wondering where Matt is this morning," he began, looking around the room with a thoughtful frown. "Well, the police, in their infinite wisdom, came and arrested him last night-"

Lizzy's gasp of shock halted Chad's recounting of the night's events as all eyes turned to the young girl. Her bottom lip was quivering and her eyes instantly filled with tears.

"Now then..." Mac patted Lizzy's arm gently, "...don't take on, it's going to be all hands on deck by the sounds of things."

"That's true," Chad nodded, and managed a small smile of reassurance for Lizzy, who he knew was especially fond of his brother. "I wanted to tell you this in person so that you wouldn't listen to the gossip that is bound to spread throughout the village," Chad explained, and Lizzy nodded, managing to swallow back her tears.

"As I said, Matt was arrested late last night – I got our solicitor to the station as soon as I could and he's fighting in Matt's corner," Chad told them. "Ferguson is damned good; if anyone can get Matt off this trumped up charge he will. But for now, as Mac said, we're going to need all hands on deck." Looking at Mac and Jackson, Chad went on to explain what he needed. "I know you've been helping Matt with the harvesting..." he began again, looking at Mac, "...do you think you could bring in the maize crops with Jackson, or do you need me to help you?"

"No, my lad and I can manage," Mac assured him.

With a sigh of relief, Chad nodded, "Good. That's very good." Then he turned his eyes to Lizzy and saw her shrink back into the settee. "Lizzy, I'm going to be relying on you to take care of the horses. I'll be able to nip down to the stables every now and then to help you out, but for the most part you'll be on your own – will you be ok?"

Straightening in her seat, Lizzy nodded and said, "I can do lots of stuff by myself now, and I don't mind hard work. But what about the riding lessons – we've got two groups booked in this morning and two private lessons for this afternoon," she informed Chad, her nervousness beginning to ebb as she realised that he was relying on her.

"Thanks for letting me know – I'll have to give that some thought," Chad told Lizzy, pleased to see that she was rising to the challenge. "I won't have time to take the lessons myself – maybe Wes or Fallon could give us a hand. I'll sort that out in a bit."

"I've got a private investigator coming to see me shortly," Chad informed them, getting to his feet and bringing the meeting to a close. "I'm going to do everything I can to get Matt back here where he belongs," he told them, looking more at Lizzy to reassure the young girl.

"Er, not to be nosey or anything..." Jackson hesitated before leaving the sitting room, "...but you didn't actually say what Matt has been charged with."

Chad looked grave and his heart lurched as he forced himself to say the awful word. "Murder – Matt has been charged with the murder of Camille Parsons and is being linked to the disappearance of Pamela Hooper."

Lizzy swayed on her feet and Jackson caught her to his side. "It's stuff and nonsense," he told her. "You know Matt could never do that."

"O.of course," Lizzy stammered. "But the police..."

"You believe them?!" Chad was angry now, after all Matt had done for Lizzy she was too damned quick to condemn him.

"No, no..." Lizzy gasped, shocked that he would think that, "...it's just...my dad...he says 'once the police have got you in their clutches they make up all kinds of stuff to keep you in gaol' – something about crime rates," she finished lamely, her eyes cast to the floor.

Realising he'd misjudged Lizzy, Chad told her not to worry about police fabricating evidence. "That's what solicitors are for, Lizzy. They won't get away with pinning this on Matt – we won't let them."

"Too damned right," Mac agreed, outraged that the police could get it so wrong. "The best thing we can do is get on with our work, Lizzy. We need to keep the farm running for when Matt comes home."

He sounded so sure that even Lizzy began to look hopeful. "I'll do my very best," she told Mac, then dared turn her gaze to Chad. "We all will."

The meeting with the private investigator went well; Chad had been left feeling more confident that his brother's future was in safe hands. *Between Ferguson and Baxter, Matt should be home in no time.*

But Chad was not a stupid man, as much as he wanted to believe that justice would prevail, he also acknowledged that what Lizzy's father had told her was also a possibility. *Especially if Swain is involved!*

It was mid morning when Fallon arrived to take the

riding lessons that were booked for that day. The Craemer's had been shocked by the news of Matt's arrest and Fallon had immediately offered to help out.

Not wanting to make things awkward for her, Chad introduced Fallon to Lizzy then quickly made himself scarce.

<u>CHAPTER SEVENTEEN</u>

I'd never been in any kind of a prison before, so sitting in the police cell gave me plenty of time to think and worry.

When I looked back at what had happened in the last few months, it all came down to me being a damned coward.

I knew how I felt about Pam, knew I wanted our relationship to get past the friendship it had been all our lives. But I had been too cowardly to make the move – worried that I might lose her for good if it all went wrong.

Even when she had been brave enough to make the move – and yes, that kiss had shaken me to my very core – I still didn't have the guts to follow through.

By then I'd gotten myself in so deep with Swain I wasn't sure which way was up! Hell, I didn't have a right to anything Pam and I might have had together; by then my yellow streak had grown to be a mile wide.

How could I tell Fenella about her father's deal without hurting her – she'd turned out to be a genuinely nice person, a gem waiting for the right man to discover her.

But that man wasn't me and her father should have known better than to try to buy love for his darling daughter. Talk about an over indulgent parent!

But what now? Camille Parsons is dead, the police think I did it and had a hand in Pam's disappearance. Looking at it from their point of view I suppose it does look bad for me.

But I don't know anything about anything; not even Pam's whereabouts. But I bet Swain knows something about everything – damn the man!

Surely he couldn't have arranged Camille's murder – that's just too idiotic for words. The man's a millionaire, a big time newspaper mogul – why would he put all that at risk by getting involved in a murder. Not just to frame me, surely – he can't be that desperate to marry his daughter off.

But Mac did say that Swain likes to get his own way.

I wonder if that's it – if the mad mogul just doesn't like to be beaten at his own game.

Giving him that money back felt good. I'll be sure not to let myself get into a situation like that ever again. I've got to toughen up with my creditors if I'm going to make the farm work — though Swain admitted having a hand in even that situation. I hate to think what he did to threaten those people into holding back payment, but that's for them to deal with.

I need to get out of here and find Pam. Maybe Isabelle and John have heard from her by now? I can't see Pam leaving them to worry without a word — not if she's able to contact them, anyway.

I've got to stay positive — I can't afford to think the worst. Pam is fine, her feelings got hurt when Swain told her all those lies about me and Fenella getting engaged, but I'll find her and put that straight.

Damn it, Pam, couldn't you have asked me before you took off to who-knows-where!

Working hard in the stables, Lizzy tried not to think about Pam being missing, suspected murdered, or Matt being in gaol for that and Camille Parsons' murder.

I just have to concentrate on my work!

Fallon seemed to be managing the riding lessons, and Mac was bringing in the rest of the crops with Jackson's help. Chad was dealing with the office work as well as trying to find Pam and get Matt out of gaol.

All in all, everyone was busy with something, which is why no one noticed when a visitor arrived.

Fenella knocked on the front door of the main house but got no answer. She walked to the largest barn and searched inside, but no one was around. Walking round to the stable yard, Fenella searched the tack room, the stalls and then walked round to the paddock where Fallon was still giving lessons, but she found no sign of Matt.

"Excuse me…" she called out to Fallon, "…could you tell me where I can find Matthias Langdon?"

Frowning over at the woman she recognised as being Fenella Swain, Fallon held a finger up to her advanced riding group and told them she would be back in a moment.

"You're looking for Matt?" Fallon looked at the young beauty with curious eyes. "I thought you two were seeing each other."

Looking uncomfortable, Fenella felt her cheeks heat and looked down at her shoes momentarily. "We were that's why I need to speak to him. Do you know where he is?"

Raising her brows, Fallon felt a lot of sympathy for the young woman – she knew what it was like to love a Langdon man and have him ditch you; it wasn't something you recovered from easily.

"I don't know how to say this without upsetting you..." Fallon began cautiously, "...but, Matt's in gaol."

"Gaol! That's ridiculous!"

"I assure you, Matt is in gaol," Fallon told the stunned young woman. "He was arrested on suspicion of murder."

Slapping a hand to her forehead, Fenella had to grip the paddock gate with an outstretched hand to save her from falling. "Matt...murder...I.I...that can't be right..."

Going quickly back to the group she had been teaching, Fallon asked the eldest girl to continue the lesson while she took Fenella up to the house.

"Come on, you need to sit down," Fallon instructed, taking Fenella by the elbow and steering her towards the house. "It's obviously come as a bit of a shock."

Fenella just nodded wordlessly, allowing herself to be towed along.

"Take a seat," Fallon instructed. "I'll get you a nice cup of tea."

But before Fallon returned Chad walked into the office and found Fenella seated there.

"What the hell are you doing here?" Chad's face was dark as thunder as he regarded the woman he considered to be to blame for his brother's imprisonment.

At that moment, Fallon returned with a cup of tea in hand and witnessed his anger. "Chadwick Langdon – don't you dare shout at that poor girl – can't you see she's in shock!"

While the two glared at each other, Fenella got to her feet and tried to leave only to faint a second later at Chad's feet.

"Now see what you've done!" Fallon quickly put down the cup of tea and crossed to Fenella's side. "You brute – you haven't changed one bit!"

Lizzy, who had come into the house behind Chad, stared at Fallon in disbelief - she didn't think anyone dared speak to Chad that way.

Scooping Fenella up in his arms, Chad strode passed Fallon and into the sitting room then carefully laid Fenella on the settee.

Feeling bad about frightening the girl into a faint did nothing to improve Chad's temper. "What the hell is she doing here – and why were you making her tea?"

Pressing her back into the wall as if to disappear, Lizzy watched in amazement as Fallon stiffened her spine and, once again, glared at Chad.

"The poor girl came looking for Matt – she had no idea that he was in police custody," Fallon informed him sharply, then turned to look at the young girl stood perfectly still by the sitting room door. "Lizzy..." Lizzy jumped at the sound of her name and looked warily back at Fallon, "…you will stay with Ms Swain and make her a fresh cup of tea when she comes round – I don't trust *him* to be civil!"

On her way to the door, Chad caught Fallon by the arm and spun her around. "Where the hell are you going?"

Wrenching her arm out of his grasp, Fallon stuck a haughty chin in the air and said, "I have a riding class to finish!" With that she was gone, leaving Chad to look on sheepishly while Lizzy tried to make sure that Fenella was comfortable.

"I don't know anything about fainting," Lizzy spoke to no one in particular then looked up at Chad with wary eyes.

"Don't look at me…" he told her, "…I don't know the first thing about women, apparently!"

Left to her own devices, Lizzy decided to sit and keep a careful eye on her charge. She didn't want Fenella to come round and find herself alone.

That would frighten her all over again!

When she did come too, Fenella was mortified at her situation and wanted to drive herself home immediately. But Lizzy had been ordered to let Chad know the minute the young woman revived and had run to tell him before Fenella could slip away.

In his usual brusque manner, Chad had taken charge, brooking no argument from Fenella when she made to protest.

"Jackson will drive your car and Mac will drive his own," Chad instructed after Lizzy had fetched the two farmhands into the office. "That way we make sure you get home safely and my men can get themselves back here to continue their work."

He might have been absent from the farm for a few months, but Chad had settled back into his old role like he'd never been away.

Later that day Chad got some good news and some bad. The bad came from the family solicitor, Ferguson. He'd tried to get Matt out on bail but had been blocked at every turn. Ferguson informed Chad that he suspected there was someone influencing that decision, but hadn't been able to get around it no matter what he'd tried.

The news from Baxter, the private investigator that Chad had hired, however, turned out to be much more promising.

"Ms Hooper used her credit card to purchase a train ticket to Essex," Baxter told Chad. "A couple of days later she used the same credit card to book a flight out to Germany – your sister, Ashton Langdon, was on the same flight."

"What?!" Stunned, Chad had to think fast. "Was it a return ticket? Do you know when, or if, she's due to return?"

"Apparently Ms Langdon is entered into an under 25s show jumping competition in Babenhausen, to which Ms Hooper accompanied her," Baxter informed Chad with some satisfaction. "They will both be returning tomorrow."

"That's damned good work," Chad congratulated the PI. "I want you in Essex tomorrow and I want Pamela Hooper to accompany you back to Dersley Dale!"

"I will certainly do my best-" the PI began, but was interrupted by Chad's outraged reply.

"My brother is sitting in a police cell — you get that bloody woman back here no matter what it takes," Chad told Baxter, and heard a 'yes sir' before his phone cut off.

Damned females! Trouble...every last one of them!

<u>CHAPTER EIGHTEEN</u>

"We've found Pam," Chad grinned at me, the two of us sitting on my bed in the police cell. "The private investigator I hired is bringing her back with him sometime today."

I was flabbergasted, but heartily pleased, and grabbed my brother in a bear hug, slapping his back hard. "I knew you'd come through for me. Where the heck has she been?"

"Went down to Essex on a train to see Ashton - then they both went to Germany for a competition Ashton was entered for," Chad explained. "I've already been on to Ferguson — he said, as soon as Pam gets back he'll have you out of here. There's nothing connecting you to the Parson's murder now that Pam has been found."

Going suddenly still, I looked at my brother through

haunted eyes. "I started remembering all those programmes I've watched – you know, the ones where people are wrongly convicted on circumstantial evidence. The thoughts going through my head were pretty scary," I admitted ruefully.

"Christ!" Chad expelled a breath, nodding his understanding. "Can't imagine what you've been through – just the thought of being locked up... Well, it would give me nightmares too, bro."

When Chad left I smiled and waved as if I didn't have a care in the world, but inside I still quaked.

I don't think I'll really believe I'm getting out of here until I walk out that door with you, Chad. But at least I have hope now. At least Pam has been found and is well, no thanks to me!

I didn't take well to being locked up. My mind was constantly going over the evidence that the police kept telling me they had – the fact that Pam was missing was the crux of their case but they said they had other things.

Ok, yes, I had known both women, but I hadn't been out with Camille in quite some time. As for the 'other' things they said they had – well I hadn't given Camille any presents, we just hadn't been seeing each other long enough for that to happen. So...they couldn't have found anything of mine on her body.

But corrupt police have been known to plant evidence and I couldn't help wondering if Swain had any on his payroll.

Ferguson said he'd been thwarted at every turn when he'd tried to get me out on bail – that must mean that some pretty influential people are in Swain's pocket. If that's true, planting evidence would be a breeze, just pay someone somewhere to toy with things just enough to point in my direction.

Good Christ, I'm going to drive myself crazy thinking this way. I have to get out of here and make an effort to make things up with Pam. She'll understand everything when I'm able to explain about Swain and his stupid idea that I marry his daughter.

Yes, she will – Pam's a good sort, I told myself hopefully, and lay back on my bed looking up at the dirty ceiling I'd done nothing but stare at since my arrest.

To Baxter's relief, Pamela Hooper hadn't put up any resistance to the idea of accompanying him back to Dersley Dale. She'd called Chad Langdon to verify who he was and the situation that Matthias Langdon found himself in, then they'd hopped on a train and were met at the station by Chad himself.

"Good to see you," Chad gave Pam a warm hug then took her suitcase from Baxter.

"How's Matt – is he still in gaol?" Pam asked, her concern gratifying considering that Chad knew his brother was in love with her.

"He is, but he looked much better once I told him that you were on your way home," Chad told her, the relief making him appear much younger than he had the past few days. "We all feared you were dead – Camille Parsons was found murdered and the police were tying your disappearance in with it – that's how they came to arrest Matt," he explained.

Feeling her cheeks heat, Pam quickly apologised. "I know it was stupid but I just had to get away. When Theo Swain told me his 'good news' I just couldn't face another day working alongside your brother – watching him take Fenella out was one thing, but to witness their engagement – well, that was the last straw."

"It's not my business to interfere…" Chad began cautiously, "…but you might want to give Matt a chance to explain. There was never any engagement – Theodore Swain has a lot to answer for!"

On the way from the station, Pam realised that they were headed towards the farm instead of her cottage.

"Would you mind dropping me off at the cottage first…" she asked, assuming that Chad had business with Baxter who was sat in the back seat of the car, "…I would really like to get settled back in?"

"No. You're staying at the farm with us," Chad told her, not a hint of a question in his voice. "Ivy cottage is too isolated – Camille Parsons' murderer is still on the loose."

"What...Chad, really...this is ridiculous," Pam protested, but could do nothing when he calmly turned the four-by-four onto the Langdon farm's long driveway.

He got her suitcase from the boot and told Baxter to wait in his office while he showed Pam to her room. Then he put a hand to the small of her back and guided a very reluctant Pam up the stairs.

"This should do you," Chad told her as he put Pam's suitcase on the unmade bed. "Sorry it isn't aired, or anything..." he told her as he crossed the room to open a couple of windows, "...but I'm sure you'll soon make yourself at home. Come down when you're ready, I need to square things up with Baxter."

With that, Chad was gone and Pam was left in stunned silence. She crossed to the bed and flipped open the suitcase. Luckily she'd just washed all her clothes after getting back from Germany, but she hadn't had time to iron them before Baxter had turned up.

Damn the man - no wonder Fallon finds him infuriating! I don't know how she put up with Chad for as long as she did, let alone consider marrying the great ape!

But she had known Chad for many years so she also knew that he acted out of genuine concern for her safety. She just didn't have to like his high-handed manner.

Getting Matt out of gaol became the top priority once Chad had settled things with Baxter and Pam had done her unpacking.

She didn't complain further, but went with Chad to the solicitor's office and then to the police station where Matt was being held.

It had taken some time and a number of telephone calls, but eventually Ferguson had been able to secure Matt's release.

When an officer escorted me through to the station's front desk, I still didn't truly believe I would be walking out of the front doors any time soon.

They were so near, yet so far away. I'd had to fill out some paperwork and had my belongings returned to me. Then I'd been shown into a small room where my brother, Ferguson and Pam were waiting for me.

Truth-be-told, this was the scariest moment of my arrest – I was dreading that a hand would slap down on my shoulder and I'd be told it was all a huge mistake – I wasn't free, I had to go back to that tiny cell and hear the key turn in the lock as I had on that first night!

Chad had me in a bear hug, and I found his strength reassuring. Then Ferguson was giving me all kinds of information, told me I needed to come and see him as soon as possible to go over everything. And then there was Pam, she was stood back against the far wall, looking at me like I was a stranger – not the look I'd been hoping for at all.

"I'm glad to see you safe and well," I told her, and Pam managed a small smile.

"I didn't realise the trouble I'd caused," she replied, her hands tucked behind her and flat against the wall to hide the fact that they were shaking.

"No worries," I dismissed easily, but the need to be out of that police station and back home on the farm was gnawing at me. "Come on, let's get out of here!"

I was surprised to find that Pam was now living at Langdon Farm. Not at all unhappy about it, but not entirely comfortable either.

Pam had got changed and gone down to the stables to see Lizzy – someone else Chad had mentioned moving into the house.

"What's got into you?" I asked Chad when we were finally alone in the office. "First Pam and now Lizzy – why?"

"With Pam, it's more a cautionary thing," Chad began,

his frown telling me that he was still straightening the whys and wherefores out in his head. "We know that Camille was murdered – we also have a good idea that it was Swain who tried to pin that on you. What I don't want to see happen…" he continued cautiously, "…is Pam doing another disappearing trick – especially not if Swain has anything to do with it – this time he might be tempted to make it a permanent one!"

"Jesus, Chad, what a morbid thought!" But I couldn't argue with his thinking. We had Pam's word that it was Swain who had told her that I was getting engaged to his daughter – which had been a bare faced lie! We also knew that he was behind the delayed payments to the farm and the bank's refusal to give us a short term loan – Swain had admitted as much to me himself. But was he actually behind Camille's murder, and would he really resort to murdering Pam just to get revenge on me?

"You need to get real," Chad said when I still looked dubious. "I had Baxter do a bit of digging on Swain at the same time as he was looking for Pam – this makes interesting reading," and he slid a type written report across the table to me.

While I read, Chad pointed out a few things for me to take note of then said, "You'll see that Swain's partner at the newspaper died a couple of years ago – according to

Baxter's sources, Terrance Manning had been planning to sell his 40% share, unhappy as he was at the way the newspaper was being run."

I looked across my desk at Chad and he nodded, giving me a wry smile. "You think Swain had him killed?" I asked.

"I think it was very convenient timing," Chad evaded. "The partnership was drawn up so that if one partner died the other's share went to the surviving partner, so as to cause as little disruption to the newspaper as possible. Of course, there was a settlement figure included to provide for the deceased partner's family, but nothing like what the share could have been sold for on the open market."

"So…Swain got rid of a thorn in his side and made a packet of money in the process," I summarised.

"He's richer than God and thinks he's just as powerful," Chad scoffed derisively. "I wouldn't put anything past that man!"

"Ok, so that's why Pam is here, but why do you want to move Lizzy in?" I asked, curious.

"The only reason I didn't suggest it before is that it would have seemed inappropriate for a young girl to be living with two single men," Chad explained. "But now Pam is here, Lizzy doesn't need to be living with an abusive father."

But I wasn't as certain as Chad seemed to be. "I'm not

so sure that Lizzy will agree," I cautioned quietly. "She looks after the little ones – I don't think she'll just abandon them on your say so."

"Don't worry about it…" Chad sat back in his chair with the air of a man who knew he would get his way, "…I've already thought about that."

He didn't explain further and I already had enough to worry about so didn't press him on the matter.

CHAPTER NINETEEN

Working with Pam again wasn't as awkward as I'd thought it might be after our strained reunion on my release from gaol.

I was on cloud nine just having her around again – that short time without her had shown me just how much I loved Pam and I would find a way to tell her that come hell or high water!

For now I have to work at getting back in her good graces. The time I'd spent with Fenella obviously wasn't going to be forgiven easily, as I found out when I tried to help with the mucking out of the stables.

"Don't you have enough to do?" Pam had asked after I'd offered my help. "I thought you were going to bring the maize crop in – Lizzy and I are perfectly capable of managing the stables."

And they were, especially now that Lizzy was living in. I don't know how Chad pulled that one off but he got his way yet again.

"Ok. Alright. I only wanted to help," I told her, but turned and walked while I said it.

I worked long hours with Mac to get the maize crop harvested, and Jackson took on the care of the beef herd and the milking of the dairy herd. I was so tired at the end of the day I would fall asleep the second my head touched the pillow – but I still managed to dream about Pam.

"Come on, Lizzy, you need to concentrate," Pam told the young girl who wasn't enjoying her riding lesson the way she usually did.

"I'm sorry, Pam, I'm trying but I can't seem to get it right today," Lizzy frowned sadly.

"Ok, we'll try again tomorrow if we get time," Pam sighed, not feeling any better than Lizzy for some reason.

I should be happy to be back, but being around Matt is making me feel miserable. Maybe I should go back to Ivy Cottage – Lizzy could come too if she wanted.

I really wish things could get back to how they were.

The tension in the air was getting to everyone. Chad spent more time in his room than he usually did – a habit he'd adopted since his return home.

Hell knows what he does up there – I don't remember

Chad spending that much time alone before he left. Probably doesn't want to be around all the misery. I just wish Pam would forgive and let live.

I was in the kitchen cooking the evening meal when the girls came in from the stables. Although Chad wasn't as useful in the kitchen, we took turns so that it didn't fall to the women to do all the cooking. After all, we'd managed pretty well before they came to live here, so it wouldn't be fair to take advantage.

"That smells good," Pam observed as I stirred a few spices into the bolognaise sauce. It was the first time she'd initiated a conversation with me, the compliment was a welcome bonus.

"Thanks – it's my own recipe," I smiled warily. "You and Lizzy get washed up and I'll have this on the table in 10 minutes."

She actually smiled – tentative, but a definite smile.

After that I made a real effort to make the meal special. I got out a bottle of wine and laid the table, then I used the house phone to call up to Chad's room to let him know dinner was on the table.

"This looks great," Lizzy announced as she walked into the dining room and took a seat. "And it smells even better." She sniffed dramatically and rolled her eyes up to the heavens. "You're a better cook than my mam, and she's pretty good," Lizzy chuckled.

I felt my cheeks heat but felt gratified that my work had been appreciated. "Thanks, Lizzy, I'll take that as the very highest of compliments."

Lizzy laughed and took another mouthful of the lovely spaghetti bolognaise.

"Have you ever had wine, Lizzy," I asked.

"Lord no – my dad would kill me," she said, looking shocked by the suggestion.

"I don't see any reason you can't have one glass if you'd like to." Chad looked up from his meal to where Lizzy sat watching him cautiously. "After all, children in Italy are allowed wine with their meals – nothing wrong with it if you drink responsibly, Lizzy. And your dad will not lay a hand on you," Chad finished, his tone brooking no argument.

Looking first at Pam for approval, Lizzy picked up her wineglass and held it out to Matthias for a taste.

"Not too much…" Lizzy held up a hand after I'd poured less than half an inch of white wine into the glass, "…I don't want to waste it if I don't like it."

But when she sipped the wine Lizzy smiled, liking the slightly sharp taste and the underlying sweetness.

She held her glass out to Matt again with a mischievous grin.

"Do I take it madam would like more?" I asked with a French accent that made her giggle delightfully as she nodded.

"And you, madam?" I turned to Pam, still pretending to be a French waiter.

Her smile was wonderful, reaching her eyes and turning my heart to mush. "That would be very nice, thank you," she nodded, and her smile actually stayed in place.

I was in seventh heaven all through the meal — we ate and chatted easily, making real progress for the first time.

Both girls insisted on clearing the dishes and loading the dishwasher as their contribution to the meal. Chad did his usual disappearing trick which left me on my own in the sitting room.

Not a bad meal if I do say so myself. And Pam's reaction made it all the more enjoyable.

"I'll cook tomorrow," Pam informed me when she walked into the sitting room with Lizzy. "It's only fair."

"Alright," I agreed happily enough, and asked Lizzy how the riding lessons were coming.

"I didn't do very well this morning," she recalled, looking a bit disgruntled.

"Why was that?" I asked, but turned to look at Pam for an answer.

"I think Lizzy was feeling a little sad this morning," Pam observed, giving Lizzy a reassuring smile. "Maybe you're a bit homesick?"

Lizzy grimaced then nodded, looking at Matt with wary lowered eyes. "It isn't that I'm not happy to be here..." she assured me earnestly, "...but I do miss the little ones – and my mam's a really nice person once you get to know her."

"I'm sure she is, Lizzy," I told her sincerely, having heard nothing to make me think otherwise. "Couldn't you give your mum a ring and ask when would be the best time to come round for a visit. Living here doesn't have to mean losing touch with your family," I reminded her.

"Really...?" Lizzy's eyes went round as saucers, her happiness evident to anyone looking at her.

"Really," I smiled, feeling happier than I had in a while. "Would you mind if I took Pam away for a little while," I asked, not sure if Lizzy would be comfortable in a strange house on her own. "Chad's upstairs if you need anything," I added when she shook her head.

"Are we going somewhere?" Pam asked when I took her hand and pulled her to her feet.

"Yes, I've got something I want to show you," I told her, but didn't expand further.

I could have taken Pam down to the south field in my

car, but decided to take the tractor as the small cab meant a cosier ride.

"You're being all mysterious," Pam commented as I climbed back up into the cab after locking another field gate behind us.

"Actually, this is it..." I smiled, watching her frown with confusion, "...this is my brainchild for ensuring the continuation of Langdon Farm for many generations to come."

I sat looking at the empty field for a couple of moments then got down out of the tractor's cab and went around to help Pam down.

She had no idea what was going on in my head, but smiled at me anyway.

I loved that smile, the way it made her eyes twinkle in the moonlight. I loved Pam, and I needed to win back her trust before I could expect her to return that love.

"Ok..." she said eventually when I didn't hurry to explain, "...you've cleared the field of livestock, but I don't see any other changes."

"Imagine all the people of our generation being able to buy or rent a house in the village – wouldn't that be a good dream to have?" I asked, envisaging how the houses would look.

"That would be amazing – I've lost a few good friends

who had to move away just to be able to get a place of their own," Pam recalled sadly. "So, you're actually thinking of building on this field."

"Not just thinking," my smile broadened. "Sykes, my builder, has already had the plans approved and I've made an agreement with the council that these homes will be affordable and for local's only. I've seen a solicitor that Ferguson recommended and he's drawing up deeds that will stipulate the houses are only to be resold to either local people or the council."

"And that's enforceable?" she asked uncertainly.

"It is if the solicitor draws the deeds up right," I told her, and was gratified to see Pam's smile broaden as she too looked around the field envisaging my dream.

"Matt, you're amazing — but what made you think of this," Pam asked with a wide sweep of her hand.

This was it, the moment I'd been leading up to where I'd spill the beans and confess all to Pam. It was harder than I'd imagined all the times I'd rehearsed this little speech in my head — but it was now or never.

"Do you remember when you and the men were worried about the farm — the finances," I added when Pam looked confused. But then she smiled and nodded as it came to her.

"Yes, I remember Mac was worried that Jackson might

be out of work again, and you know what it's like getting a job around here," Pam's smile turned rueful.

"Yes, well, it was a close call there for a while," I admitted. "And yet I needed to find the money to hire a stable hand to help you out – the one part of the farm that was taking off better than expected was the riding stables. You've built on what Ashton began and turned it into a little goldmine," I said, full of admiration for the hard work Pam always put in. "And I think Lizzy is working out well, isn't she?" I asked, knowing full well that Pam enjoyed the girl's company and was grateful for the hard work she contributed.

"Lizzy is a wonder," Pam praised her young apprentice. "She's a natural with the horses and will be a good rider when she learns to relax a little. In time, Lizzy will be able to help out with the riding lessons – taking the beginners classes to start with – but not for about a year, I'd guess."

"Have you mentioned that to Lizzy?" I asked, wondering how Lizzy would take that kind of responsibility. She'd been frightened of her own shadow when she'd first come to Langdon Farm, but had come out of her shell as time went on.

"No, I don't want to rush her – Lizzy just needs a bit of careful handling," Pam told me, and I nodded in agreement.

"Well, I'll leave that for you to decide – the stables are your domain," I told her. "And that reminds me, now that we're more financially stable; I'm giving you a decent raise."

"You are?!" Pam's face lit up in the moonlight, her eyes bright with happiness.

"I told you I would," I reminded her and thought, *Christ I want to kiss you right now – just to feel you in my arms again and know that you belong there.*

I shoved my hands into my jeans pocket to stop from making a grab for her; Pam looked too damned tempting by half!

"Yes you did, and you're nothing if you're not honest," Pam stated quietly. "Was that all you wanted to tell me?" she asked, the sideways tilt of her head telling me that she knew there was more to it.

"No, not really," I began again, somewhat nervously. This explanation could make or break us and I wanted to get it right. "You know the farm has been in our family for generations…" I asked, and Pam nodded that she did, "…well I almost lost it – back when Mac was worried for Jackson's job. He had every right to be worried – I was scared witless," I confessed, rubbing a hand nervously at the back of my neck.

"But you kept saying everything was fine," Pam

remonstrated mildly. "I knew things were worse than you were letting on!"

"Yes, well, I didn't want to admit that I'd made a hash of things. I wanted to be as good as Chad," I confessed.

Taking a step nearer to me, Pam put a hand on my arm and sent shivers all the way down my spine.

I took her hand and began walking the empty field, staying close to the road so as to keep the light. It felt so good to have that small contact – I never wanted to lose it ever again.

"He was a tough act to follow," I continued eventually. "But it has always been my dream to run Langdon Farm, and I nearly lost it."

"But you didn't," Pam reminded me gently.

"No, I didn't." I winced at the thought of what I'd agreed to in order to save the farm and swallowed hard before telling Pam all about it. "I got in a real mess with the books – I didn't want to push for payments when I knew the farming industry as a whole was going through tough times – but I let it get out of hand. I was getting letters demanding payment for supplies and equipment I'd bought, but I wasn't getting the money in to allow me to settle up." I sighed heavily, "Like I said, I got into a real mess."

"So what did you do?" Pam asked, knowing this was the crux of the matter.

"First off I tried to get some money in from those who still owed us," I told her. "But I just kept getting the run around. Then I went to the bank – Carl Morrison, the manager, has known my family for many years and, at first, it seemed like he was going to help me out." My expression hardened as I remembered the about turn the man's attitude had taken after the telephone call that I now knew was from Theodore Swain.

"I don't know how he knew I was there or what I'd gone to the bank for, but Theodore Swain called the bank as I sat talking with Carl – after taking that call Carl couldn't get me out of his bank quick enough," I growled angrily.

"But if the bank didn't help you out, how…?"

Pam allowed the question to tail off, some inkling of what I'd done beginning to dawn on her.

"I was completely out of options – I thought, for sure, the farm would be taken from me," I recalled, and felt a shudder course through my body at the memory. "And then I found Fenella waiting for me beside my car. I must have looked a mess – she wouldn't let me leave without telling her what was wrong. And that's where I got the idea of going to her father for a short-term loan," I finally admitted.

Seemingly trying not to think badly of me, Pam

nodded as she thought about that. "Doesn't seem unreasonable – he's mega rich and Fenella obviously suggested he'd be open to the idea," she mused, rationalising my actions.

"Yes, it seemed to be the only course of action open to me – but I should have known it was too good to be true," I added bitterly.

"It was…?" Pam encouraged me to continue.

"I don't know why or where he got the idea, but Swain got it into his head that I was the right man to marry his daughter," I told her, forcing the words out through clenched teeth.

I heard the gasp as Pam took in that information and knew she would probably despise me for my weakness.

"I couldn't lose everything my family had built up over all those years," I pleaded quietly. "I had to agree to court Fenella, without letting on that it was part of an agreement with her father, and marry her if that was her eventual wish."

I couldn't look at Pam; she continued to walk quietly by my side but her hand fell away from mine and I knew I'd lost her.

CHAPTER TWENTY

We continued to live and work together, sharing meals and various chores, but the atmosphere had changed.

Pam still managed a smile or two, even chatted about things that were going on in the stables or some progress that Lizzy had made that she thought I would be interested in, but she was distant.

For me, the physical nearness of her was torture. My body ached to hold her, responded to her womanliness in ways that were difficult to hide. I needed Pamela Hooper with a passion that was driving me insane.

Yet I tortured myself needlessly – found reasons to be near her, to inhale Pam's unique fragrance so as to remember it for the times when I had to be away from her.

I probably looked like a love-sick puppy the way I trailed after her. But Pam didn't seem to notice, just kept on doing what she was doing and smiling and nodding in all the appropriate places.

So near yet so far away from where I needed her to be. I had to find a way back into her affections or die trying.

It was Chad who eventually tore my thoughts away from my obsession with Pam. His news was shocking and I gave it my full attention.

"Another woman has been found murdered," he declared after calling me into the office. "I didn't want to tell you out there; the girls won't have heard the news yet and I didn't want to frighten them unnecessarily.

"Yes," I agreed dully. "Do we know her?"

"I don't think so," Chad shook his head. "Baxter has contacts in the local police force – he told me her name is Melody Celestine, 26 years old and from a neighbouring village. The police haven't officially released her identity, so keep it under your hat for now. I'm more concerned with keeping the girls safe – no trips into the village alone until this creep is caught, right?!"

"I didn't realise you still had Baxter on our payroll," I told Chad, watching him carefully to assess his explanation.

"He's just doing some work for me – so he's on my payroll, not the farm's," he informed me tersely.

"Your payroll? And how are you going to pay for that – you won't take anything from the farm," I told him.

"I have means of my own," Chad confessed cryptically. "I wasn't living on the streets while I was away."

"So you got a job?" I asked, genuinely interested to learn what kind of work he'd picked up.

"In a way. All you need to know is that I don't need the farm's money and I can take care of my own needs quite adequately," Chad dismissed with a tone of finality. "I've already called Wes with the news – he'll be watching out for Fallon and their mother, making sure they don't go anywhere without him – so they should be safe."

"Must chafe a bit not being able to take care of Fallon yourself," I said, knowing how I'd feel if Pam's safety were in another person's hands.

"Wes will take good care of his family," Chad declared, trying to convince me, and no doubt himself, that he wasn't at all worried about Fallon.

I went back to work after filling Mac and Jackson in about the latest murder, asking them to keep a particular eye on the women.

When I got back to the stables, Pam was already taking a group riding lesson. I stopped to chat with Lizzy and helped out with some of the work.

"Did you give your mother a call?" I asked Lizzy as I undid a fresh straw bale and we both began laying it on the clean stall floors.

"I did," she smiled broadly. "She said the best time to visit with them would be tomorrow in the morning. Dad's on an early shift," she added by way of explanation.

"Do you mind if I come with you?" I asked, and Lizzy looked surprised. "I'd like to meet your mother, she sounds nice."

Looking pleased at my interest, Lizzy nodded enthusiastically. "She'll like that — but don't wear anything special, the young'uns are dab hands at getting jam, or whatever else they've got on their hands, all over people."

"Alright, we'll leave around 9 if that's alright with your mum," I suggested. "Maybe you ought to give her another call to let her know."

"Oh. Yes."

Lizzy looked hesitant, somehow unable to make a decision.

"What's wrong?" I asked, concerned.

"It's just...well...my dad's on an early today as well," Lizzy began to explain.

"And you'd rather call your mother while he's at

work?" I asked. "Go up to the house…" I told her when Lizzy nodded, "…if Chad's in my office use the telephone in the sitting room."

"But, what about my work?" she asked, chewing on her bottom lip.

"I'm here, I'm working, nothing is falling behind," I told her, and shooed her away.

"Thanks, Matt."

Her grin was shy yet happy and I watched as Lizzy actually skipped her way up to the house.

Oh to be that young and carefree again.

But I couldn't moan – I had the farm, the one thing I'd always longed for. If I could have Pam too then I'd be living the dream.

By the time Lizzy returned the riding group were leading their horses back to the stable yard and we took them from them.

All the stalls now had clean bedding laid so, one by one, we took off their saddles and led them back into their own stalls.

The three of us worked well together, rubbing down the horses and cleaning off the saddles and tack.

Pam and Lizzy were finishing off Symphony when I heard Lizzy tell her that I was going with her to visit her family tomorrow. "My mam was really impressed," Lizzy enthused to Pam. "She said as he must be a very good boss if he cares enough to be interested in an employee's family."

I listened harder to hear Pam's reply and wasn't disappointed.

"I'm sure your mum is absolutely right – Matt is a very caring boss, fair minded and not at all rigid," Pam stated. "Though he does expect us all to work safely, so there are certain things that we all need to remember – like not going into Ronan's stall or, if you need to leave early let someone know that you're going so that we're not searching for you thinking you might be in a ditch somewhere."

Lizzy laughed at that idea but assured Pam she would. "They're very different…" I heard Lizzy say.

"Who is?" Pam asked.

"Matt and Chad," Lizzy clarified. "Chad scares me."

Pam had obviously smiled, I could hear it in her voice when she answered.

"Chad's not so bad – he was always getting into trouble when we were kids," she told Lizzy, making the young girl giggle.

"I can't imagine that," Lizzy admitted. "Now if you'd said Matt-"

"So, you think I look like trouble do you?" I asked as I

walked up to Symphony's stall and stood by the half gate.

Blushing at being caught talking about me, Lizzy smiled shyly. "I can imagine you being a bit like my little brothers, they get into everything – I can't imagine Chad as a boy at all."

I laughed, pleased that Lizzy felt at her ease with me. "I assure you, my brother got into his share of trouble. Chad and Wes were demon children – I didn't get my behind wacked until I got big enough to hang around with them. Trouble, the pair of them, my mother always said."

I was pleased to see that Pam, too, was smiling at the memories and continued to reminisce just to keep that smile on her lovely face.

"And Pam wasn't always an angel either," I grinned, and laughed when she frowned, giving her head a discreet shake to stop me from telling any embarrassing tales. "We used to have a dog, Shane, an Alsatian, and Pam loved him." I watched her cringe, though her lips were trembling with the effort to contain a smile, knowing which memory I was about to recount. "It was a really hot summer and the five of us were playing in the back garden when my dad came out with the hosepipe. Chad and Wes had on swimming trunks, Fallon and Pam just kept their knickers on and I was running around in the nude, apparently."

Lizzy let out a lovely giggle and Pam's smile finally won free. "We were about 3 or 4 at the time," Pam inserted with a roll of her eyes.

"Anyway…" I continued as if Pam hadn't spoken, "…madam here decided she was going home and taking Shane with her, so when we weren't looking Pam managed to wriggle under the fence and Shane just jumped it and went with her."

Looking shocked and worried, Lizzy turned to Pam and said, "You must have worried them sick. My brothers have given me the slip before, when I took them to the park; I nearly died of fright till I found 'em!"

"You're right, Lizzy. When my parent's realised that Pam was missing dad and Mac went out looking for her. They found her by calling to Shane; he let out a couple of barks and moments later they found Pam holding his collar and walking towards the farm gates. She'd lost her knickers during the great escape and was covered in mud where she'd wriggled under the fence. My dad hosed her down again when he got her back into the garden."

Pam tutted and pretended to be annoyed, but Lizzy was almost bent double with laughter.

"We had a lot of fun back then," I mused, looking wistfully at Pam.

"Yes…we did," she smiled sadly.

And we will again, I thought with determination. *I will earn your affections and your love if I have my way!*

While Lizzy finished off with the horses, Pam and I worked on the tack. She was standing in the far corner, right where I'd decided I needed to be, and I reached over her to put a set of reins back and get another set down.

I heard Pam's sharp intake of breath as my body brushed against her. "Sorry, won't be a sec'" I told her, but took my time and held her trapped against the wall.

My heart was pounding and when I dropped my arms I rested my hands on her shoulders, outwardly gaining my balance, but inwardly I was savouring the closeness.

When she looked up, Pam's eyes didn't seem to be in focus and she didn't pull away from me.

I wanted desperately to claim her lips, to feel them yield under my own, but Pam wasn't ready, I knew that. Pulling back from that moment was one of the hardest things I've ever done, sheer torture in the extreme.

"Sorry," I apologised, and like to think I saw disappointment come in to her eyes as I moved away.

For the rest of that morning I made one excuse after another to get close to Pam and, after a while, she didn't bother to move out of my way. I even fancied that she put herself where she knew I would need to be, but maybe that was just wishful thinking on my part.

When, finally, I couldn't find any more jobs to do in the tack room, I had to force myself to leave.

"I could do us all some lunch if you and Lizzy want to come up to the house," I offered, hoping to get more time with Pam.

"I made sandwiches for me and Lizzy this morning," Pam replied, and I swear she looked as disappointed as I felt.

"Oh, alright. I'll catch you later then," I told her, but my feet still didn't move.

"Matt, I-"

Pam was cut off by Lizzy's bright and breezy voice telling her that she had finished her jobs.

I looked at Pam for another long moment, and then I turned on my heels, striding up to the house with leaden feet.

I didn't look back, but I felt Pam's eyes on me until I rounded the corner of the stable yard out of sight.

CHAPTER TWENTY-ONE

The visit with Lizzy's family went well. Her mother was very welcoming and the two boys were as well behaved as any 4 and 6 year olds could be.

"I hope our Lizzy is doing good work…" her mother said when she returned with a tea tray laden with homemade biscuits, "…we brought her up not to be lazy and she always helped out where she could when she was at home."

"Lizzy is a gem," I smiled, and looked over at the young girl who was blushing wildly. "I know Pam has counted her blessings since she joined us."

"Pam – that's the stable manager, is it?" Mrs Collier asked looking at her daughter then back at me.

"Yes, mam," Lizzy answered. "Pam's ever so nice – she's teaching me to ride and everything."

"Yes, so you told us before," Mrs Collier frowned. "Do you think it's safe for Lizzy to be riding horses?" she asked, turning back to me.

"It isn't without its dangers," I admitted seriously. "But I believe you've got more chance of being injured crossing the road than riding a horse with the proper safety gear on. And Pam really is an excellent instructor," I added to reassure the woman.

"You really like it there then Lizzy?" her mother asked, and when Lizzy nodded enthusiastically she seemed appeased. "Well, that's good — that's really good. It's a rare pleasure to work at something you love doing, and Lizzy has always loved animals."

"Lizzy is a credit to you," I told her. "I've rarely met a more polite young lady — we just need to feed her up a bit."

Mrs Collier nodded and sighed. "She takes after me for that, I'm afraid. The only time I had any weight on me was when I was carrying the children — it fell away the minute I gave birth."

"Some women would say you were lucky," I observed with a smile.

"They would..." Mrs Collier agreed, "...but I don't care for being skin and bone but there's nothing to be done about it. I eat just as well as our Lizzy does, it just doesn't seem to stick to my bones."

She chuckled then and put a gentle finger under her daughter's chin to lift it. "You're a pretty young thing – you take care not to catch the eye of any young men – there's time enough for courting in a few more years."

"Mam!" Lizzy gasped and her cheeks flamed with embarrassment, flicking to look at me under her lashes.

"Your mother's right, Lizzy," I told her. "We'll be keeping a watchful eye on your daughter, Mrs Collier, don't you worry."

"Thank you, Mr Langdon," and Mrs Collier rested back in her chair with her cup of tea.

As we left the house, Lizzy kissed the boys goodbye, telling them that she would visit again soon. Then she kissed her mother and the two had tears in their eyes when they parted. "I'll see you soon, mam. Mr Langdon gave you the farm's phone number if you need me for anything."

"Yes, you get on now and don't keep Mr Langdon waiting," Mrs Collier told her daughter as she shooed the two little boys back into the house and closed the front door.

"She'll be crying now," Lizzy informed me once we were both seated back in the car. "I've never been away from home before."

I wasn't sure what to say so stayed quiet and left Lizzy to her thoughts.

Once we got back to the farm I gave Lizzy some work to do to take her mind off of being homesick then went into the office to get some of the dreaded paperwork done.

Bloody office work – it's the one side of running the farm that I'd gladly hand back to Chad. But it doesn't look like he'll be staying long – he and Fallon don't seem to have made any headway. They're both such strong minded people – neither one will want to admit they were wrong or just give a bit of ground. But I can't talk, my relationship with Pam couldn't get any worse if I tried.

Deep in invoices and bookkeeping, Matt didn't realise the passage of time until his stomach started to rumble. He lifted his head and sniffed the air then realised there was a wonderful aroma coming from the kitchen.

He got up, walked through the dining room to the kitchen and got the shock of his life.

Lizzy and Pam were cooking up a storm – steam was rising from a saucepan of boiled rice and the most delicious aroma was coming from a wok that he didn't even know they owned.

"Ten minutes," Pam told me when she saw me standing in the doorway. "Lizzy, how about setting the dinner table?"

"No. No." I protested. "You two have done enough, I'll set the table."

My mouth was watering at the thought of what we would have for dinner. *Heaven knows where they got the ingredients, Chad and I certainly didn't buy them.*

While the girls dished up, I went to shout Chad down but he was already coming down the stairs.

"Did you take cookery lessons while I was away?" Chad asked as he descended the last few stairs.

"Not me this time, bro," I told him and chuckled at the thought of me taking cookery lessons. "The girls have cooked something very special if the smell of it is anything to go by."

It was – hardly a word was spoken at the dinner table – we were all too busy eating to speak.

"Oh my lord," Chad rested back in his seat with a hand on his sated belly. "I can't remember when I last had a meal like that one. Lizzy, if I get down on bended knee, will you marry me?"

We all laughed, including a very red faced Lizzy, but she told him, "You might want to aim that proposal at Pam – she did most of the actual cooking – I just helped prepare it."

Without setting a single brain cell into gear, I responded to Lizzy's suggestion with a deep frown at my brother. "Don't even think about it!"

A hush fell over the room and I would have gladly

bitten my tongue out there and then. But there was no taking it back, so I just rolled with it.

I gave Lizzy a wink and began collecting up the dishes, "You know that's why Chad has you both secreted away here, right? He never did like my cooking."

The atmosphere was broken and Lizzy got up to help me take out the pots, then suddenly we were all on our feet and clearing the table.

"Ok, everyone out of the kitchen and I'll make some coffee and bring it in the sitting room," I told them once the table had been cleared. But when Pam made to protest I didn't stop her.

"Let me help," she told me and I just nodded.

We didn't speak, at first; I loaded the dishwasher while Pam got out the mugs and put the kettle on.

"Have you seen anything of Fenella lately?" she asked quietly; so quietly that I turned to see if she was crying.

"No, and I don't intend to change that situation," I told her honestly.

"Oh."

We carried on with our jobs, both dying to say something but saying nothing at all, until Pam dropped a bombshell.

"She came here, you know," Pam told me, and turned to lean her back against the work surface.

I stood up and looked at her, a quizzical frown over my eyes. I didn't pretend not to know who she was talking about and simply asked, "When?"

"I wasn't here at the time – it was while you were in gaol," Pam told me. "It was Lizzy that told me about it, but I spoke to Fallon as well and she said Fenella fainted when Chad told her that you were being held at the police station, under arrest for murder."

"That thick-headed dolt!" I sighed heavily, hands on hips and shaking my head at my brother's insensitivity. "Was she alright?"

"Fallon said she got Chad to put her on the settee and she left Lizzy to watch over Fenella till she came round. Then, apparently, Chad took her home," Pam recalled what her friend had told her.

I nodded, looking at Pam speculatively. "Why tell me? Do you think I'm interested?"

Pam lowered her eyes and took a moment to answer. "I don't know why – I suppose I wanted to see if you were."

"Damn it, Pam – I made an honest mistake when I was out of my mind with worry," I told her, not happy that she was holding this against me. "I was never interested in Fenella – even she sensed that after a couple of dates."

"She did...?"

"Yes, she did," I confirmed and took a step closer to Pam without making to touch her in any way.

"Oh."

"Oh," I repeated, but smiled down at her with all the love I had inside for this woman shining in my eyes for the world to see. "I've never been interested in anyone but you – not since I saw you running around the yard with nothing but your knickers on while my dad hosed us all down."

Returning my smile with her head cocked to one side, Pam looked up at me. "We were 3," she told me.

"I don't care – you were always the one for me and you always will be." I took another step closer to the woman I loved and hoped she wouldn't reject me.

Then I did the most impulsive thing and, before I could think better of it, I dropped down to one knee in front of Pam and took her left hand.

"Pamela Mary Hooper, I love you more than life, I need you more than my next breath – please, I'm begging you, will you marry me?"

The world stopped turning, my heart stopped beating and even the dust motes stilled. Time was suspended until I heard Pam speak.

"I will."

Those words were the most precious sounds I'd ever

heard and it took me a moment to believe I'd heard Pam utter them.

"You will...?" I gasped, then got hurriedly to my feet. "You will," I repeated, now smiling maniacally and holding her shoulders firmly.

"Yes..." she laughed nervously, "...I will."

When I took Pam in my arms and kissed her a cheer went up from the dining room - Lizzy and Chad had been listening in and were happy for us.

"About bloody time!" Chad stated loudly. "Now, maybe, you'll stop mooning about the damned place."

I wasn't even tempted to answer him – I had the woman of my dreams in my arms and she'd just consented to be my wife.

"You won't change your mind when you've had time to think about it, will you?" I asked, still not able to believe it was really going to happen.

"I won't change my mind," Pam assured me. "But you have to promise to talk to me from now on – no more secrets or trying to cope on your own – we're going to be a team," she stated firmly.

"Agreed."

EPILOGUE

Chad knew that once his brother's engagement to Pam became public knowledge, Swain would come after Matt with a vengeance.

But Chad was already prepared for that scenario and collected together all the information Baxter had gathered on the man and his business dealings. After copying it all, Chad parcelled it up and posted it off to the Metropolitan Police in London, as that is where most of Swain's business dealings were carried out.

He knew it wouldn't be long before Swain was interviewed – though he doubted they'd have much luck in making any of it stick. Swain was the original 'Teflon man'; he paid others to do his dirty work.

But it would take Swain's mind off his brother, and that was the main aim.

Chad considered Matt to be too naïve for his own good, but he knew how men like Theodore Swain worked. He'd made it his business to know all about men like Swain – it had made Chad's crime thrillers believable and had earned him a lucrative publishing contract.

But that's another story.

*****

If you have enjoyed this book, please leave a review at the place of purchase. Thank you.

www.ingramcontent.com/pod-product-compliance
Lightning Source LLC
Chambersburg PA
CBHW070626170726
48291CB00003B/895